Donl

In

Uncharted

Waters

By

Perry Comer

In Memory

And

Honor

Of

The Seventeen Seaman

Of the USS Cole

BOOKS BY PERRY COMER

The Prize
(Donland)

The Messenger
Donland and the Hornet

Donland's Ransom
Donland and the Hornet

Raid on Port Royal
Donland and the Hornet

The Bond of Duty
Donland and the Hornet

Siege
Donland and The Hornet

The Rescue
Donland and the Hornet

Donland's Courage

Donland's Victory

Fall of Fort Fisher
(Juvenile action/adventure)
(Civil War)

Andrew's War
(Juvenile action/adventure)
(Civil War)

Fighting Marines: Hardy's Commission

Fighting Marines: Hardy's Challenge

Chapter One

"She's still there, no gaining just keeping pace with us," Powell said with irritation in his voice.

"Aye," Donland replied while holding to the railing, gazing out at the white-capping sea. He added, "We'll not know her intentions until we are nearer our destination."

"Have you determined her nationality," Major Dormer asked.

Donland faced the major. "I've not, but in these waters she could be any one of several. I'll not speculate; doing so is utterly useless. We are at peace and I can only assume that whatever vessels I encounter are observing the peace. Spain, France and Portugal each have a number of men-of-war sailing these same waters. So, as I said, it does no good to speculate. The world has changed with the coming of peace and we find ourselves in uncharted waters."

Major Dormer did not reply. He turned his attention to the group of soldiers gathered on the forecastle. Beyond them, past the bowsprit, the transport *Jersey* bore half of Dormer's regiment.

She, like *Oxford*, plowed her way through the waves, throwing spray high above her bows.

Oxford crashed into another swell, green water with white froth washed onto the foredeck. Donland was reminded of a cold icy voyage to Nova Scotia when ice hung so thick on the rigging that many lines parted from the weight of it. But here, hundreds of miles off Brazil, there was no ice, just nine to ten foot swells constantly battering *Oxford*'s hull. It was not a sea for the faint of heart or for an aged rotting ship. There was more than two feet of water in *Oxford*'s well and the pumps were in continual operation.

The bell struck six strikes sharp and clear. "The glass is turned!" Midshipman Mellencamp called.

"Enter it in the log, Mister Mellencamp," Andrews barked.

"We've another five hours of daylight," Powell observed.

"Aye," Donland acknowledged. He chose to say no more but instead turned his attention to the set of the mizzen sails. "What of the wind, Mister Winslow?" he asked.

"Same as yesterday, Captain, will hold till sunset then slacken a bit," Winslow answered from his perch on the chest.

"Mister Powell, attend the muster, I will be in my cabin," Donland said.

"Aye, Captain," Powell replied.

Honest followed Donland to the cabin. Rowland, his cabin steward, met them. "Your coat, Captain?" the steward asked.

"Aye and I'll have coffee," Donland answered.

"Aye," Rowland said as he helped remove Donland's soggy coat.

Before sitting at the table, Donland glanced at the barometer. He mentally noted than it was unchanged in the last two hours.

Rosita, his cook, smiled as she sat a pot of coffee, a cup and a small dish containing a pastry in front of him. She did not speak and returned to the galley. He smiled as he remembered his promise to set her ashore, pleased with himself that he did not. He knew that a woman aboard tended to lead to complications and was considered bad luck. One woman and just over three hundred men was certainly a mixture for trouble. On the other side of the ledger, however, was Rosita's husband, a member of Andrews' watch. He bore the brunt of the difficulties.

Donland eyed the pastry; it wasn't like any other he had seen. It was a swirl with a white coating. He lifted it, sniffed it and took a small bite. It tasked of cinnamon and orange. *Truly remarkable!* He was tempted to take another bite but chose to have the coffee.

"You look pleased," Honest observed as he sat.

"Aye, this pastry is remarkable."

Honest smiled and replied, "Aye, I'd a bite of one earlier. Mind you, only a bite for that was all she allowed me."

"She's quite the cook," Donland said as he lifted the pastry.

Honest nodded and said, "I've a word with the bo'sun like you told me. He said the matter of the boy is settled. Mister Brunson was agreeable to having Worth in his watch. That will be an end to it."

"It better and I'll hold you to it. I'll not have the likes of him fomenting trouble below decks. Were it not for your intervention, he would have received twenty-four so mind you, I'll not refrain again."

"Aye, Sir, and I'd not ask you to do so again. He's given me his word that he spoke the truth."

"His word against the boy's," Donland reminded Honest.

"Aye, that is true," Honest agreed.

Donland drank the remainder of his coffee. Outside his door the men were assembling for the afternoon muster. *Oxford* dove into another swell.

"Getting rougher if I'm to judge," Honest said.

Donland grinned, "Mister Winslow advised me that the further south we go the larger the swells. There may be some as high as twelve feet, even larger beyond the Falklands. I've heard tales that south around Cape Horn, they can reach forty feet."

3

"Bloody fools that want to live on a rock in the midst of such seas," Honest said.

"Whalers go to where the whales are. And, if they are in such seas as this, then that is where the whalers go. I'd not care for the life."

"Nor, I," Honest remarked and stood.

A knock at the door sounded.

Donland called, "Enter!"

The door opened and Powell came in, removing his hat as he did. "Muster completed, Sir, wind holding," he said.

"How much water have we?" Donland asked.

"Just over two; pumps are keeping it at bay. Mister Brunson reports no problem with the pumps," Powell answered.

"Any change in our companion?" Donland asked.

"None," Powell said as he eyed the pot.

Donland smiled and refilled the cup, "You may as well sit and drink."

"Aye, and gladly," Powell said as he sat and laid his hat on the deck. He asked, "Do you remember what occurred this month six years ago?"

Donland's face was blank. "I think not, last year is difficult enough to remember."

Powell grinned and said, "I would have thought you would have remembered. It was six years ago that our fortunes changed. I was so angry at the time, I'll not forget you telling me that you were to command *Morgador* and I was to remain aboard Medusa. Captain Okes threatened me with charges of insubordination when I broached it with him."

Donland smiled, "Aye, I remember the event just not the anniversary. Six years, you say?"

"Six," Powell said and added, "and an eventful six it has been."

"That is so. We've both fared well, have we not?" Donland asked.

Powell lifted the cup and sipped coffee. His eyes shined with memories. "You advanced from midshipman to post and I from first to first. But, I've no complaints for were it not for you I would not have held my first command."

"You miss her?" Donland asked.

"Aye, more than I should. Thus far, command of *Stinger* has been the high point of my life and career." Powell caught himself, "Not that serving as your first is any less, ah er, rewarding."

Donland and Honest both laughed at Powell's difficulty. Powell's face reddened with embarrassment.

Donland regained control and said, "James, I too know what it is to lose that first mistress. When *Hornet* was taken from me I thought I'd never walk the deck of my own ship again. And even though I command here, my feelings for her have not dissipated. I've heard it said that a man's first command gains his heart for all his days. I believe it to be true."

"Aye," Powell said in agreement.

Donland changed tack, "Is the major still on the quarterdeck?"

"Gone below," Powell said and added, "He seems to be spoiling for a fight."

"Aye, his kind always are. Bloody fools care only about glory. They can lose the whole of their commands and care not one whit as long as they can claim a victory. And if they should lose, the blame will fall elsewhere." Donland said with distaste. He'd seen officers like Dormer, hated them for their willingness to send men to die for no worthwhile gain.

Powell downed another swallow of coffee then said, "I'll be glad to set him ashore on that rock and set sail with a fair wind for warmer waters. I confess to wondering if his assignment was due to the ruffling of feathers."

"Most likely, the ruffling of petticoats," Honest said with a grin. "His lads say that he always has an eye out for the ladies and cares not if they are wed or not, much like our new surgeon."

5

The conversation was not to Donland's liking, "Three more days and we will reach the Falklands. Once there, Major Dormer will no longer be our concern. Until such time, he is due respect and courtesy as is Doctor Trammel."

"Aye," Powell said and asked, "What of our sailing companion, she's sailed in our wake for a day. Every tack we make she has made. It seems to me that she has ill intentions. Have you decided on a course of action?"

Donland blew a breath then said, "I agree that her movements, were we at war, would signal ill intent. However, we are not at war and our actions must not provoke a reaction. We will maintain our course and watch her. If she intends to interfere in our task then, and only then, will we take appropriate action. As long as she maintains her distance we will do nothing."

He stood, and as he did Powell reached for his hat. Powell stood and said, "I believe her to be French."

"Speculation will gain you nothing, Mister Powell. If you consider that France is bent on ruling the whole of Europe you would conclude that they would not waste an asset such as a sizable frigate this far south. And by that reasoning, not speculation, I conclude her nationality to be neither French nor Spanish. Therefore, her nationality will remain in question."

"I'd not considered that line of thought," Powell confessed.

Donland half-smiled and called. "Rowland, I'll have my hat and coat, if you please."

"Aye, Captain," Rowland responded and came from the sleeping compartment with a dry coat and hat.

"Are you going on deck?" Powell asked.

"No," Donland answered as he slid an arm into the coat. "I should take a turn about the lower decks and then will return here to go over accounts with Mister Leeland. You may accompany me if you wish."

"I think not, Sir, I'd best be present on the quarterdeck while our shadow is about," Powell answered.

All ports on the lower gun deck were shut tight with double lashings against the high seas. The air was foul, but it could not be helped as long as the sea ran high. The continual clanging and clanking of the pumps could be heard above the hub-bub of the many voices. Soldiers lay sprawled in almost every space, forcing Donland and Honest to either step over them or between them. Honest led the way with a lantern to the next hatch leading down to the orlop deck. As they descended the ladder the combined smells of unwashed bodies, damp wood, mold, and the filth of the bilge assailed their nostrils. Added were the odors of rancid butter and cheese from the purser's stores.

"Dry," Donland said as they moved along the passage past the various lockers pushing past idle soldiers

"Aye, the old girl is bearing up," Honest replied.

David and Simon were the only two occupants of the midshipman's berth. David was to have the next watch and Simon had completed the earlier watch. They sat on their chests playing whist. The mess boy, a small fellow not more than ten, stood over the table watching.

David caught Donland's eye and immediately jumped to attention. His coat was hung on a peg, as was his hat. A shock of black hair was draped over the scar on his forehead. Simon was also hatless and coatless.

"I'd have thought you so proud of your new station in life that you'd not ever take the coat off," Donland teased the boy.

Simon grinned broadly, "Aye, Captain, I confess to being proud of it, but not half as much as my Da."

"Aye, that is so," Honest said.

"Such as it should be," Donland said and smiled. "He'll swell like a toad when the day comes for you to sit for your examination."

"Aye, Sir," Simon replied and added, "But David will do so long before I do."

David brushed back his hair just enough that it did not cover his eye.

Donland studied them for a moment and thought how much they had grown in the last year. David was slightly heavier but the same height as Simon. "Another year, perhaps, what say you David?"

"I wish that it were tomorrow, I'm ready but I know that it will be at least another year," David answered.

Donland nodded and said, "Just bear in mind that believing you are ready and being ready are not always the same. You've more experience than most your age and I would have you at my side no matter the circumstances. However, you've yet to stand alone with no other resources but your wit and strength. When you've such a test, then you will know in your heart that you are truly ready."

Simon asked, "Sir, did you have such a test?"

"As a middy, yes," Donland began. "I was in charge of a watering party of ten men set ashore in Africa. Midshipman O'Hara, a year my junior assisted. We were attacked by a band of natives. I had my sword, dirk and one pistol. O'Hara also had his sword, dirk and a pistol. When they came from the bush throwing spears, O'Hara went down leaving me alone to command. I fired my pistol, picked up his and fired. By then they were on us and it was thrust and parry. I ordered the men to the boat but two stayed by my side and we held them and managed to escape."

"Were you wounded?" David asked.

"Aye, as were several others. Good men died that day, including Mister O'Hara. I still fault myself for not being able to recover him."

"But you were able to save those under you," Simon commented.

"Aye, six of us survived, but just." Donland said and paused. He said gravely, "Such a test will come to both of you and afterwards, should you survive, it will remain with you and be as clear as if it were no more than an hour ago. In the future, you'll have other occasions when you will face dire circumstances and in those times you will draw courage from that first test."

"How old were you, Sir," David asked.

"Your age, just past my sixteenth."

Overhead there was the rumble of cannon being rolled to the ports.

"That will be Mister Malcolm exercising the starboard guns," Donland said as he looked up at the deck beams.

"Late in the day for drills?" Honest asked.

"Aye," Donland acknowledged. "I should return to the quarterdeck."

Chapter Two

Donland stepped from the great cabin to a dark slate gray morning. The low clouds warning of rain to come. Powell was on the quarterdeck waiting.

"She's still there, more distant, but still there. I would hazard a guess that she encountered some difficulty in the night," Powell said.

Donland did not inquire about *Jersey*; she was as before darkness fell under light sail, maintaining her distance ahead of *Oxford*. "Any signals from *Jersey*?" he asked.

"Only the recognition," Powell answered.

Donland turned about and inquired of Winslow, "What of the wind?"

Winslow shifted his girth from the locker and stood. "Squalls making up and I'd say a bit more wind before the rain. Might see snow before it leaves us. It will not hazard us, and will stay about as is once the squalls have finished. It will all be over before nightfall and after that I expect some clearing."

Donland glanced at the sky and then to the set of sails. They were on a south by southeast course with only topgallants and topsails.

"Hold course, Mister Powell, and perhaps a reef in the topgallants if there is more press of wind," Donland ordered.

"Aye, Captain," Powell answered then asked, "Shall I drill the gun crews this afternoon?"

Donland considered the question then answered, "If Mister Winslow's weather predictions are correct, I should say not. The rolling of this sea makes exercising the crews dangerous. If the waves grow higher, we will lose good men to injury for no good purpose. Malcolm and Brunson can set the men tasks below deck. Also, advise Major Dormer to keep his men below. Send a signal to *Jersey* that she should also keep the army below deck."

"Aye, Captain," Powell said.

The day wore on, the sea becoming more boisterous and savage. The only bright spots of the day were the brief moments it did not rain.

Donland stood staring out the transom windows. Occasionally, he picked up the small glass and trained it in the direction of the unknown sail. She flew no flag at her gaff and was still there, well aft, and on a leeward tack. Her continued presence troubled him, but there was nothing he could do but watch.

Rowland sat brushing a pair of boots, Honest sat with his feet braced against rib and appeared to be asleep. *Oxford* pitched to and fro as she thrust forward into the oncoming swells. Both Rowland and Honest seemed totally unaware of the continual motion.

He put away the telescope and sat at the table. The book Betty had given him lay open, and he began to read the ancient tale of Homer, but his mind shifted to Betty. She had laughed and said that when the days were long and he was bored, he could turn his thoughts to something worthwhile. But the truth was that the only worthwhile thing to think about was Betty.

Beyond his door, there was the single clanging of the ship's bell and the hurried shuffle of feet. He was tempted to go on deck but restrained himself. Darkness would fall soon and with its coming would come the long night. For the married men, it was the most difficult time to be a sailor. For a single man, the night was for playing cards, singing or for sleeping. For the officers nights were the lonely times, because unlike the hands, the officers did not enjoy such camaraderie as that of the gun deck.

He grew bored with the book and laid it aside, stood and took up the small telescope again. The distant sail was like a nagging sore that would not heal. He mused again of her nationality and intention. Night was falling quickly, but he could still manage to see her topsails. He fully expected that her captain would close the distance before nightfall. There would be a half-moon in the evening hours if not hidden by cloud, which would allow her to continue to close the distance.

"Honest, let us go on deck," Donland said.

Honest did not stir. So, Donland shouted, "stand to!"

Honest slowly set his feet on the floor before looking at Donland and said to him, "you don't need to shout Captain, I heard you the first time," in a voice that reflected more humor than irritation.

Rowland quickly put the boots down and began gathering Donland's coat and hat.

"Something amiss?" Honest asked.

"Nothing as yet," Donland said as he allowed Rowland to help with the coat. "Time will tell if there truly is something amiss and if I have missed something that I should have seen. Go on deck and pass the word for Mister Powell, if you please."

"Aye, Sir," Honest said as he started for the door.

Andrews and Mellencamp had the watch. The sky was beginning to clear and there were patches of blue overhead. Winslow had been correct in his assessment of the weather.

"What of the wind, Mr. Andrews?" Donland asked.

Andrews was quick to respond, "South by East, Sir," the young lieutenant managed.

Donland gripped the rail and examined the set of the sails. Powell joined him, but did not speak.

"Let us go up to the poop," Donland said to Powell.

"Aye," Powell responded with the hint of question in his voice.

Donland did not speak as they climbed the ladder. He carried with him a telescope in order to observe their shadow.

"You have a growing concern about our shadow?" Powell asked.

"I do," Donland said as he lifted the telescope to his eye. "I think I know his intent."

"You believe he has decided on a course of action?" Powell asked.

Donland found the sail. She was maintaining her distance. He lowered the glass and turned to Powell, "I'm sure you have given thought to our shadow and have come to some conclusions. I should like to hear them?"

Powell grinned and began, "Just another vessel en route to a destination but cautious and fears getting too close to us. That is why she maintains her distance."

"I too thought that but since she is a ship of war and her nationality is not revealed, her presence is more than coincidence. I would venture that her captain intends to sail ahead of us and block our entrance into the harbor."

"Surely not, such would be an act of war," Powell stated.

"Aye, it would. Are you aware that France has agents in this hemisphere and that alliances are being made?"

"No, I'd not given thought to such," Powell said with surprise.

"Commodore Pettibone told me to be aware that such possibilities might come to fruition and to be on my guard. I'd not considered the possibility until that ship continued in our wake. If Portugal has entered into an alliance or if some other nation has done so, they may have orders to stop the landing troops in those islands. If so, that could be accomplished by sailing ahead and attacking *Jersey* under the cloak of darkness. There would be no war, for there would be no one to identify the attacker. A frigate, such as the one in our wake, could do so in the night. She certainly has the wind and the speed to do so, do you agree?"

"Aye, but she is no match for our guns," Powell stated.

"But more than a match for *Jersey!*"

Powell understood. "She means to sink *Jersey?*"

"Aye, I would wager that is her intent. The moon will rise before ten and will provide sufficient light for the maneuver. Until then her captain will remain in our wake, keeping close watch on our lights. He has remained on our leeward quarter in order to set all sail and far-reach both *Oxford* and *Jersey* while we are under light sail for the night. Then he intends to have *Jersey.*"

Powell nodded, "Aye, it is what I would attempt. Lulling my adversary into a sense of ease and then spring my plan. Have you a plan of your own?"

Donland held out the glass, "Study her for a moment with a critical eye."

Powell took the glass, steadied and squinted. After a full minute, he lowered the glass. "I don't see anything amiss."

"Nor should you," Donland said. "What I see is a frigate sailing with reefed sails with the wind up her skirts. Her captain is having difficulty holding back a race horse that wants to run."

Powell lifted the glass, found the frigate and replied, "Aye!"

"Let us return to the quarterdeck," Donland said.

"We will have a long night," Donland remarked as they regained the quarterdeck. "Send to *Jersey*, to lie-to, if you please," Donland ordered.

"Aye, Captain," Powell answered.

"Mister Welles, pass the word for Mister Winslow to come on deck!" Donland ordered.

"Aye, Captain!" David answered

Donland stood with his hands clamped on the railing, looking up at the first stars of night beginning to appear. He also noticed that faces on the quarterdeck were becoming indistinct.

"*Jersey* has acknowledged," Powell said in Donland's ear.

Donland lifted the glass and focused on *Jersey*'s transom. Two lights showed in her window. He lowered the glass as Winslow asked, "Captain?"

"Very good of you to join us, Mister Winslow. I've ordered *Jersey* to show two lights in her transom, get a fix on them if you please."

"Aye," Winslow said and steadied himself.

"Have you the bearing?" Donland called to Winslow.

"Aye, Captain, we will be up to her leeward quarter in less than a quarter-hour once she spills her wind."

Donland lifted the glass again. The lights were extinguished.

"Mister Powell douse all lights!" Donland ordered.

"Aye, Captain!" Powell answered and began giving orders.

Donland knew what he was about to do was dangerous. To come alongside *Jersey* was difficult enough on a calm sea but in such high seas in the dark risked damaging both vessels. With the two lights showing briefly in her transom, *Jersey*'s captain understood that he was to lie-to and show no lights. Only the occasional clang of the ship's bell would allow *Oxford* to judge distance. The two ships would then lie-to about three chains from one another.

"Moon coming up!" Powell said.

"Aye, we will know soon if my assumptions were correct," Donland said.

A bell clanged off *Oxford*'s starboard beam.

"We've room enough not to worry. *Jersey* is a bit ahead of us." Donland stated.

Powell did not reply but stared into the darkness. The night sky was filled with clouds hiding the stars.

They waited together for half-hour and neither spoke. *Oxford* was like a ghost ship, the men were forbidden to move about except when necessary to attend the needs of the ship. Voices were not to get above a whisper or there would be punishment.

The eastern sky brightened as a cloud uncovered the moon. The sudden burst of light spread out like a fan across the sea. The frigate was to leeward, coasting along under light sail. Donland lifted the night glass and put it to his eye, "Two miles distance, she's setting her topsails and royals!"

"Her captain will see that we are lying-to," Powell said.

"Aye, but it is too late for him to change his tactics. He is forced to sail on. He'll not have a chance at sinking *Jersey*," Donland replied.

"He'll be waiting for us when the sun rises," Powell stated.

"Yes, and he will know that he will have to face our guns and risk war if he fires. He'll not be anxious to do so. His only other choice will be to gain the weather-gauge and come at us as we are tacking to enter the anchorage. Even then, he'll receive a good amount of damage. It will be a risk he will have to weight."

The clang of *Jersey*'s bell rang out, perhaps closer than before.

"Shall I signal *Jersey*?" Powell asked.

"Aye, show two lights. We've nothing to fear from our shadow now," Donland said.

Powell started toward the ladder, then stopped. He asked, "Did you recognize her?"

"I believe her to be the Portuguese forty-two gun *Liberal*. When I last encountered her, her captain was named Cabral. That was back when I commanded *Hornet* and rescued the prince. He will remember me and his hatred of me will not have lessened."

"Aye," Powell said and sought the ladder.

Jersey showed the required two lights.

"Steerage, Mister Winslow?" Donland called.

"Aye, Captain, just," Winslow answered.

"That will be sufficient for now, and then we will put her under light sail for the night," Donland replied.

He turned to Powell, "I've need of your speaking trumpet. I will attempt to speak with Captain Cunningham."

Powell produced the trumpet and Donland climbed the ladder to the poop. He put the trumpet to his lips and called, "Ahoy! *Jersey!*"

There was no answering call, so again he shouted into the trumpet, "Ahoy! *Jersey!*"

Still there was no answer, so he tried a third time. This time a faint voice called back, "Ahoy! *Oxford!*"

Donland felt a tap on his arm and turned. Honest said, "Let me, Captain."

Donland handed over the trumpet. "Tell them light sail."

"Aye, light sail," Honest answered and bellowed without the trumpet, "Set light sail!"

Someone with equal lung capacity shouted back, "Light sail!"

Without prompting, Honest shouted, "Aye!"

The answer came back, "Aye!"

"Well done Honest," Donland said. "Let us return to the cabin for a tot."

"Aye, that will do me," Honest replied and followed Donland down the ladder.

Powell was waiting. "Shall we beat to quarters?" he asked.

"I think not, *Jersey* is safe and our Portuguese friend will not attempt anything in these high seas and so little moonlight. At first light, set an extra man in the crosstrees to keep watch," Donland said then asked, "Join me for a tot to warm your blood?"

The moon chose that moment to duck behind a cloud. Powell answered in the dark, "I think not, but thank you, Captain. I've the next watch."

"Then I shall see you at first light," Donland replied and started for his cabin.

Rosita prepared breakfast for Donland consisting of eggs, bacon, potatoes and fresh baked bread. While eating breakfast his mind was on the frigate. He was not conscious of having consumed every scrap of food until there was no more. Pushing away from the table, he stood and accepted the conclusion he had reached. The frigate would no longer be within sight; she would be waiting to spring a trap. He pushed away from the table and stood.

"Rowland, I will go on deck," he called.

"Aye, Captain," Rowland answered as he came from the sleeping cabin with Donland's hat and coat.

"Has *Jersey* a lookout in her crosstrees?" Donland asked as he passed the helm.

"Aye, she has two," Powell answered.

Donland nodded and asked, "Has she sighted the Portuguese?"

"Captain Cunningham has not reported having done so," Powell answered and added, "but I'm sure that he will see her before we do if he continues to sail ahead of us."

"Aye, that is so, signal *Jersey* to go about and to sail in our wake. I would rather not chance some trickery drawing us away so that she can be attacked. We will be nearing the Falklands by sunset."

"And you think we will land the troops some time after sunrise?" Powell inquired.

"If we are not challenged," Donland replied. "We will know more before the sun sets if we remain vigilant."

Powell took a step closer to Donland and asked in a whisper, "Have you a plan?"

"I have and I believe it will be to your liking," Donland whispered back.

He then said in his normal voice, "Set all the sail she will bear. Instruct *Jersey* to do likewise and to remain aft of us."

"Aye, Captain," Powell said.

"Mister Winslow may I have the pleasure of your company in the chart room?"

"Aye, Captain," Winslow said as he heaved his bulk from the sea chest.

The chart was already laid out on the table. Donland removed his hat and unbuttoned his coat. Winslow bothered with neither.

"I would have your opinion, Mister Winslow. See here," Donland said as he pointed to the chart. "I expect the frigate we encountered during the night to be waiting for us in the vicinity of Sedge Island. It is my intention to sail directly to this point, five miles north of the island, and then draw the frigate further east. *Jersey* is to remain over the horizon to our west and once the frigate begins to shadow *Oxford*, Captain Cunningham is to sail close to Carcass Island and into Byron Sound. Once there, the troops can be landed at Port Egmont. *Jersey* will be unprotected, but as long as she remains undetected, I believe her journey can be completed without incident. Providing the water around the island is sufficient. What is your opinion?"

Winslow studied the chart and said, "There will be enough water under her hull. The danger to her will be making the tack to enter the channel. I would expect the wind and the waves to be contrary and should the sea be exceptionally high, she may broach."

"A risk that will have to be borne," Donland said and straightened.

Winslow rubbed his chin.

"A thought, Mister Winslow?" Donland asked.

"Aye, they be soldiers and used to the land and marching, might they land here," Winslow pointed to a spot on the map, "and go overland rather than risk the channel?"

Donland again bent over the map, "Aye, a walk of no more than ten miles. But I don't know the terrain."

"Barren and rocky," Winslow ventured.

Donland considered the trek. It was reasonable; Major Dormer would think not. But the safety of his troops should be foremost in his considerations.

"Once we've drawn the frigate away we will go about and land the remaining troops."

"What of Major Dormer," Winslow asked.

Donland answered with a half-smile, "We will lie-to and I'll have Captain Cunningham aboard to explain the plan. The major will accompany Captain Cunningham back to *Jersey* and remain aboard her for the landing of his men."

"He'll not like that," Winslow said and grinned.

"No, he will not," Donland mused.

Oxford dove into another roller, throwing spray high into the air. Overhead, the sky was slate gray without any traces of sun. The biting wind rattled blocks and tackle, and the shouts of the men working high up on the masts were carried away by it. Their work was tedious as they fought against not only the wind but the hard canvas.

"Send to *Jersey*, if you please Mister Welles, captain repair onboard," Donland ordered.

"Aye, Captain," Welles answered and opened the flag locked.

Turning to Powell he ordered, "We will lie-to Mister Powell, spill our wind and brail up the mains!"

"Aye," Powell answered and lifted his speaking trumpet.

To Simon, Donland said, "Mister Vickers, My compliments to Major Dormer, I desire his presence on deck."

Simon instantly replied, "Aye, Captain."

Donland watched as men assembled on deck and began to haul lines to first spill the wind from the sails and to brail up the mains. He waited until the tasks were completed then ordered, "Reef topsails!"

To Winslow he said, "Just enough to maintain steerage!"

"Aye, Captain," Winslow answered.

"Captain Donland," Dormer said to Donland's back.

Donland turned, "Ah, Major Dormer, thank you for coming on deck. We are going to lie-to and await Captain Cunningham. I will go over my plans with the pair of you once he is aboard. The Portuguese frigate has caused me concern."

"How so Captain Donland?" Dormer asked.

Donland did not mince words, "She intends to interfere with the landing of your troops. Therefore, I will be altering our plans for the landing."

"But she but one shall ship, certainly not your equal," Dormer pointed out.

Donland half-smiled, "That is so and were it not for your troops aboard I'd not hesitate to render her a floating hulk. But, as I have so many of your men below, there would be a risk. One I prefer not to take in these heavy seas."

"But you have the transport; between the two vessels there are more than enough cannon to sink her if she interferes."

Donland was growing irritated and said, "And put more of your men at risk, I think not. There are over six hundred men crammed into this hull and just one shot bursting through a gunport could kill upward of twenty-five men. It would be foolish of me to engage, and foolish to put all these men at risk. As to guns, the *Jersey* carries eighteen six-pound cannon and the range of those guns is half what the frigate carries. And, her maneuverability is that of a cow while the frigate's is that of a race horse. She would be useless and vulnerable and I'll not risk her."

"*Jersey*, has acknowledged!" David said.

"Aye," Donland replied and said to Dormer, "I will explain my plans in detail when Captain Cunningham is aboard. You will be accompanying him back to his ship."

Dormer blustered, "I demand to know for what purpose?"

"Major, as I explained, you will know my plans when Captain Cunningham is aboard. Now see to your preparations!"

"I must protest, Sir,"

"Must I have your escorted below?" Donland asked firmly.

Dormer turned sharply on his heel.

Chapter Three

Oxford rocked wildly as the huge rollers lifted her hull and passed underneath.

"Captain Cunningham's boat crew will have difficulty tying on to the chains," Powell remarked to Donland.

"Aye, not a sea for the faint of heart. I'd not have him aboard were it not necessary," Donland stated.

"You are concerned about the *Liberal*'s intentions?"

"Aye, there is more at work here than I was led to believe. If she has been dispatched to stop us from landing troops, then in all likelihood others are tasked with the same purpose. Only time will tell but I'll not be caught with my knickers around my ankles."

"Nor, handicapped by Major Dormer," Powell said with a grin.

"Aye, you understand." Donland replied while watching a boat being lowered from *Jersey*.

Jersey's crew lowered her launch over the side. It was, to Donland's mind the wisest choice considering the state of the sea. A crew of twelve descended her hull to take their positions at the oars and Captain Cunningham followed.

"Mister Powell, have the side manned, if you please. Let us render proper honors to *Jersey*'s captain."

"Aye," Powell answered and lifted his trumpet.

The marines filed up the hatchway ladder and onto deck before Powell completed giving his orders. There was some jeering from the soldiers but it was quickly laid to rest by a few sharp words from Lieutenant Andrews.

The side party was quickly in order but waited as the launch struggled to make the short crossing. Twice the boat was almost broached, and the crew fought a desperate fight to keep it from capsizing. Everyone in it was soaked to the skin.

Honest whispered to Donland, "I've hot rum on the brazier."

"It will be appreciated," Donland whispered back.

"Stand to!" Powell shouted as the launch banged alongside *Oxford*'s hull. Seconds later, Cunningham's hat showed above the salleyport. The marine drummer began beating his rat-ta-tat and the bo'sun's pipe twittered.

Donland was pleased with the rendering of honors. He had sworn to himself that no captain boarding a ship he commanded would be slighted as he often had been. Spite and jealousy were to be beneath any officer wearing the king's uniform. He'd not tolerate it on his ship.

Cunningham responded in appropriate navy tradition and doffed his hat to the flag and then to the quarterdeck. Donland stepped forward and extended his hand.

"Dismiss the side party, Mister Powell!" Donland ordered and said to Cunningham, "Join me in my cabin, if you please, Captain Cunningham.

"Aye, Sir," Cunningham said and followed Donland. Behind them came Powell, and Lieutenant Simons of the *Jersey*.

Cunningham was a dozen years older than Donland, a bit shorter and a good fifty pounds heavier. He was as some would say, powerfully built, with a large chest and shoulders.

Rowland entered the cabin carrying a tray with six pewter mugs and a tall steaming pot. He was followed by a boy carrying four white towels. "I've ordered hot-buttered rum and towels" Donland said to Cunningham. "I observed the crossing to be difficult. I'd not have ordered it were it not of the utmost importance."

"Aye," Cunningham said as he removed his hat and took one of the towels. "The rum will not come amiss."

Rowland poured rum into the mugs and began passing them out. Donland did not care for rum but accepted a mug and sipped. The others did likewise.

Cunningham cupped the warm mug with both hands. He said, "I would venture the meeting has to do with the frigate."

"It does," Donland confirmed. "But, not just with the frigate, I expect we shall encounter other opposition. That is why I requested that you come aboard."

They were interrupted by a knock at the door. Major Dormer entered without being summoned. He was followed by one of his lieutenants named George. Both men had the courtesy to remove their hats.

Donland did not show his irritation but said, "Good of you to join us Major. Would you have some rum?"

Dormer shook his head then remembered himself, "Thank you for your kind offer but, thank you, no."

"Then, gentlemen, let me outline what we are to be about," Donland said and moved to the dining table that held the maps and charts he would be using. "Gather round," he said.

They each moved around the table to view the map. "Here," Donland said and pointed, "are the Falkland's, and here is Sedge Island where I anticipate *Liberal*, the Portuguese frigate will be waiting. From this vantagepoint she can intercept either *Oxford* or *Jersey*. I do not wish to fight her for fear of losing a good portion of the soldiers. Therefore, Captain Cunningham, you will remain well out of sight and *Oxford* will sail ahead. Once *Oxford* is sighted, I will draw the *Liberal* to the east. A signal will be sent to *Jersey* and she will proceed westward to Carcass Island and make her way to Byron Sound and round to Port Egmont. If she is unable to enter the channel, then she will set Major Dormer's command ashore on this headland. It will be less than an hour march to the fort. Meanwhile, *Oxford* will come about and make directly for Byron Sound. The *Liberal* will surely pursue but *Oxford*'s guns have more reach and more metal. *Liberal*'s captain will take pause before interfering."

"Then why not pursue her and sink her now? Best be done with her!" Dormer questioned.

Donland looked up from the map. "In these seas she has the advantage of maneuverability. Also, be aware that my lower-gun deck would be awash and we'd sink if I tried to use those guns. So, I have limited firepower and hitting her would be difficult. I do not wish to expend a great deal of power and shot attempting to do so. I would rather have her come to me and on my terms."

"Aye," Cunningham inserted.

"Your orders state that you are to land my men at Port Egmont. I think anything less would result in charges being brought," Dormer stated with all the haughtiness of the nobility.

Donland eyed Dormer with a cold stare and said, "You will be landed. What you choose to do after that is your choice. But know this; I will not sacrifice my ship or my company for your comfort or your glory."

"Your attitude is insolent!" Dormer shot back.

"Perhaps, but yours is insubordinate. It is I who command here and my orders take precedence. Do not impede me Major or you will find yourself facing charges. Do I make myself clear?"

All eyes turned to Dormer. He answered weakly, "You are clear, Sir." More forcefully he added, "I was merely reminding you of your written orders from your commodore."

Donland held his tongue in check and addressed Cunningham, "Post two men high in the trees as we approach Sedge Island, instruct them to watch for my signal and for any sail. I will not draw away the frigate until I know *Jersey* is not in danger."

"Aye," Cunningham answered. "And what signal should I hoist if there are others about?"

"Enemy in sight," Donland answered.

"Captain Donland, surely you do not believe the Portuguese have sufficient forces in these waters to attack the transport?" Dormer asked.

"I do because Commodore Pettibone confessed to me that France has sought alliances with the Dutch, the Spanish and the Portuguese which includes the navies of the colonies. The only nation not in alliance or being courted for an alliance is the United States. They, though, are sympathetic. We must, therefore, view all approaching vessels with suspicion."

Cunningham nodded with understanding and said with a grin, "I best keep my powder at hand and my lads sharp."

"Aye," Donland replied, and asked Dormer, "Have you your dunnage ready to go across?"

Dormer pursed his lips. It was plain to everyone that the man was not pleased. "I have," he answered.

Bill Freedman called down from to the men in the fighting top and a man called down to the deck, "Sail!"

Every man on the quarterdeck instantly craned their necks to see which way Bill pointed. His outstretched arm pointed in the direction of Sedge Island.

"Right where you said she would be," Powell stated.

"It is where I would be," Donland said with a half-smile. "Mister Vickers bend on the signal to *Jersey* to proceed."

"Aye, Captain," Simon answered.

Donland ran his eyes across the deck. "Mister Powell, if you please, send Mister Welles to the cross-trees and have him take a glass. His young experienced eyes will tell us if in fact it is the Portuguese frigate."

Powell lifted the speaking trumpet and shouted to David.

The young Midshipman turned and shouted back, his words were lost in the wind and the numerous sounds of a ship at sea.

"*Jersey* has acknowledged," Simon announced.

"Aye," Donland said and ordered, "Captain Cabral will have seen our top's'l's by now and will have a good hand in the trees to identify us. Prepare to tack due east Mister Powell, let us see if the bait is taken.

"Aye, due east," Powell said and asked, "Shall we let out the topsail reefs?"

"No, but once the tack is completed if our friend wishes to give chase we will oblige him," Donland answered. He turned his attention to David who had reached the cross-trees. The young man, hatless and with his hair tied back into a que lifted the telescope to his eye. A little more than a minute passed before he called down to the men in the fighting top and a man relayed the call, "*Liberal!*"

"We will hold this course until we are a mile and a half from her. By then, her captain will wonder what we are about. I hope he will conclude that *Jersey* is just over the horizon and on a parallel course to *Oxford*. Once he decides on a course of action and sets his sails, then we will lead him on," Donland ordered.

"Aye, and by then it will be too late for her to make an attempt at *Jersey*," Powell said with understanding.

"Call all hands, if you please Mister Powell, let us be ready to go about when the time comes," Donland said and pulled a glass from the rack.

Powell lifted his speaking trumpet and began shouting orders. Men poured up the hatches to take their stations.

"Shall I send the soldiers below?" Powell asked.

"Aye," Donland answered as he studied the distant ship. She was also on an eastward tack under topsails and mizzen only. "Waiting," he said more to himself than anyone. He grinned.

"Mister Powell, have Mister Welles come down and take his station," Donland ordered.

"Aye, Captain," Powell answered.

"I make the distance about a mile and three-quarters, do you agree Mister Winslow?" Donland asked.

"Aye, Captain, about that," Winslow answered and said, "She'll have no problem getting after us."

Donland grinned again and said, "Her captain will plot an intercept course and once he closes the distance will luff and sail aft of *Oxford*. He'll feel he's been made the fool when he discovers *Jersey* is not just over the horizon sailing parallel."

Winslow chuckled and replied, "Aye, and well he should."

Donland turned to Powell, "I believe a tack to the north is in order, if you please Mister Powell."

"Larboard tack, Captain," Powell replied and lifted his trumpet. "All hands prepare to tack to larboard!" he shouted and waited until the message was relayed to the foredeck. Seeing all were in their places and ready he turned to Winslow, "Helm hard over, if you please Mister Winslow!"

"Aye, Winslow answered and prodded the two helmsmen.

Powell lifted the speaking trumpet and bellowed, "Larboard tack!"

Lieutenants Malcolm, Brunson and Andrews instantly begin issuing orders to their watches.

"Sheets haul!"

"Tacks and sheets!"

"Mains'l haul!"

"Castoff bow lines and braces!"

Whipped by the wind the sails cracked like gunshots. Pulley blocks rattled against masts and yards adding to the confusion of sounds.

The tack was completed in record time but Donland did not notice; his eye was focused on the frigate. Several minutes passed before the frigate's captain made his decision and did exactly as Donland expected.

"Mister Powell, send Mister Andrews below. I'll have the starboard ports opened! We'll give that captain something to contemplate!"

"Aye, Captain!" Powell answered.

The frigate began to come on. The distance closed to three-quarters of a mile. It was then that the frigate's ports opened and her guns ran out.

"Shall I beat to quarters?" Powell asked.

"No Mister Powell, I will keep him guessing for a bit longer as he intended for me to do."

"Mister Vickers, take a glass and go to the masthead, spy out *Jersey*," Donland ordered.

"Aye, aye, Captain," the boy answered with glee and snatched a glass from the rack.

"Mister Winslow, three points to larboard if you please," Donland ordered as he watched Simon climbing the shrouds. The boy was agile and lively as he swung himself up and over the maintop and continued to climb until he reached the crosstrees. Simon paused and pulled the glass from his shirt. He found *Jersey*; she was well west and south of *Oxford* about to disappear over the horizon. He pointed in her direction and called out, "Sou'east!" The call was relayed to the deck.

Donland smiled to himself and called to Powell, "Wear ship, Mister Powell, we will go about!"

"Aye, Captain," Powell responded and lifted his trumpet.

Donland noticed that the Portuguese frigate took that same moment to alter her course in order to pass aft of *Oxford*. She would have to alter course again to avoid *Oxford* as *Oxford* wore ship.

He continued to stare after the frigate as *Oxford* began her turn. It was not until the frigate was within two hundred yards that she turned away to pass astern of *Oxford*. He estimated that by the time the frigate was able to wear ship and give chase that

Oxford would be more than a mile ahead and *Jersey* would be in the channel readying her boats to unload the soldiers.

"She didn't fire a shot," Winslow said.

Donland answered, "Aye, and his not firing answered a nagging question."

"You were concerned that war was declared?" Powell asked.

"Yes, Mister Powell, and I have my answer. We should have no interference with our task. The frigate will follow but we have nothing to fear from her. Pass the word to Lieutenant George to come on deck, if you please."

"Aye, Captain," Powell said and ordered Mellencamp to go below in search of the army lieutenant.

The frigate wore round and continued to shadow *Oxford* as she followed in *Jersey*'s distant wake.

"Deck there!" the lookout bellowed from the top. "Three sail one point off the bowsprit!"

Donland pulled a glass from the rack and scanned the sea. He spotted *Jersey* easily enough and refocused to see topsails of two smaller vessels. He turned his attention back to *Jersey*; she appeared to be lying-to near inshore. "What the blazes!" he exclaimed and made for the poop ladder to get a better look.

"Sir?" Powell called after Donland.

"Hold course, Mister Powell," Donland said over his shoulder as he mounted the ladder.

Those on the poop instantly moved from the railing. Donland steadied the glass he carried against the railing to peer beyond the bow without obstruction of the shrouds. There was no mistake; *Jersey* was firing while lowering her boats. The two smaller sail appeared to be small sloops, and they were also firing.

He hurried back to the ladder and ordered, "Beat to quarters, Mister Powell! Signal *Jersey*, enemy in sight!"

"Aye, Captain!" Powell replied and shouted through his trumpet, "Beat to quarters!"

Mellencamp and Lieutenant George came up the hatch to the confusion of the ship preparing for battle.

George asked Donland, "You send for me Captain?"

"Aye, Lieutenant, prepare your men to disembark."

"Yes, Sir!" George answered.

The marine drummer began to beat and pipes shrilled.

"Enter it in the log, Mister Mellencamp!" Powell ordered the midshipman.

Donland returned to watching the three vessels. The sloops appeared to be anchored in the small channel to prevent *Jersey* from entering and proceeding to Port Egmont. Rather than force the issue with the sloops, Cunningham had chosen to off load the troops on the headland.

"Frigate is opening her ports!" Powell shouted.

Donland stated calmly to Powell, "Two small vessels are anchored in the channel and *Jersey* is off-loading the troops." He studied the frigate a moment and ordered, "Load and run out the forward two starboard long-nines. When we are in range, I'll have a ball in each of those sloops!"

"Aye," Powell said and asked, "What of the frigate?"

"Prepare and run out both stern-chasers. If that fool dares to fire on us hit him hard!"

"Aye, I'll pass the word to Mister Andrews and to Mister Hornsby!" Powell said.

"Reef mains'ls Mister Powell," Donland said and in the next breath, "Hold course Mister Winslow!"

"Aye, Captain!" Winslow answered and heaved his bulk from the chest to stand beside the helmsmen.

The distance between *Oxford* and *Jersey* was no more than a mile and near on a mile and a half to the two sloops. Still, Donland was not surprised when one of the forward long nine's fired. The shot would have fallen harmless into the sea but it would gain the attention of not only *Jersey* but of the two sloop captains.

Donland turned to check on the frigate. She was three-quarters of a mile behind and holding course. Her captain's intent seemed was merely to shadow. Her open ports a bluff.

Oxford's bow rose and crashed through a wave. At the height of the rising of her bow, Andrews fired the second nine. The shot tore through the fore-course sail of the nearest sloop.

"Hit her!" David said as he lowered his glass.

"Are you certain?" Donland asked.

"Aye, Captain, punctured her fore-course," David answered.

"Note it in the log, Mister Mellencamp, sloop of unknown nationality hit by long shot."

"Aye, Captain," the boy said obediently.

"The other sloop is getting underway!" David announced with the glass still to his eye.

BOOM! Andrews's first gun fired again.

"Missed," David said aloud seconds later. He followed the announcement with, "Second sloop is getting underway!"

"Mister Vickers, my compliments to Mister Andrews and have him secure his guns. Tell him well done!"

"Aye, Captain," Simon answered and set off.

Oxford was just off *Jersey*'s larboard quarter. Donland could discern no damage to the transport. "Mister Powell, we will lie-to if you please. Spill our wind and prepare to lower boats."

"Shall we secure from quarters?" Powell asked.

"No, we will remain at quarters until we've set the army ashore. There'll be enough light to do so and the army can fend for themselves for the night."

"Aye, Captain," Powell answered and began barking orders.

The frigate closed her port and began to tack.

"So our shadow has had enough," Donland said to David.

The two sloops were beating their way into the narrow channel. No doubt they too were aware their efforts had failed. What concerned Donland was who sent them to interfere with the landing of the troops.

"We have delivered our charges and are free to return once we have taken off those of Port Egmont that are to return to Antigua and any dispatches," Donland said to Powell over their evening meal.

Also, in attendance at dinner were lieutenants, Andrews, Malcolm and Brunson. The meal consisted of a slab of beef covered in carrots, potatoes and onions. Rosita prepared rice pudding for after the meal. The wine flowed with ease as did the conversation.

The question unasked was "who attempted to prevent the landing?"

Donland pondered that question while the others bandied small talk.

"Was not luck," Andrews boasted when Brunson had suggested the shot that punctured the sloop's sail was just that.

"Skill," Andrews stated, "something that is highly lacking amongst our peacetime navy if I'm any judge."

"There are more than enough seasoned officers afloat," Brunson surmised.

"Aye, but how many can shoot?" Andrews asked with a wide grin. He continued, "Laying a gun and with just the right charge, timing the motion of the ship takes skill and experience. Captain Donland can attest to that."

Donland sipped his wine and was about to take a bite of potato. He said, laying the potato back on his plate, "What you say is true, Mister Andrews, but even a blind hog finds the occasional tuber. He has all the instincts, the tools," Donland twitched his nose. "And, fortune has placed him in the right spot. So, it is only natural he should enjoy the meal."

Andrews blinked and said, "Sir?"

Powell laughed and replied, "What he is saying is that even with all your skill, you were lucky."

"Here! Here!" Brunson agreed as he hoisted his glass.

They each drank. Donland skewered his potato.

"Are we to bring more troops?" Malcolm asked.

"That is unknown, Mister Malcolm," Powell answered. "As you gain more seniority, you will come to understand that their lordships do not tip their hands. Orders from on high are not shared with captains of ships. No, we are told only when to fetch and carry not why."

"You've had a command?" Malcolm asked.

Donland chose to answer, "Aye, he has, and he distinguished himself. He had the honor of commanding his majesty's sloop, *Stinger*. Sadly, she like my *Hornet* was sold off as the Admiralty decided to reduce our strength. Commander Powell was reduced in rank and cast on the beach with so many others. Only by providence do we have a deck under our heels. As I said, even a blind hog has good fortune once in a while."

"Then Sir, we do not know what our next task will be once we return to Jamaica?" Brunson asked.

"That is so, Mister Brunson, our orders are as I said, to take off those to return with us and report to Jamaica. From there we may be tasked with either patrol, or to act as shepherd for other transports. I'll not know until I'm told, just as you'll not know what tasks Mister Powell has for you until he tells you. For now, however, let us enjoy this meal and our time together."

"Here! Here!" Powell added and lifted his glass.

Chapter Four

The following morning, with *Jersey* in tow, *Oxford* entered the channel between Keppel Island and Saunders Island. The channel was a welcome departure from the heavy seas and both ships anchored in the relatively calm waters of the roads.

"The gig if you please, Mister Brunson," Donland said just after the bell struck six in the forenoon watch.

"Mister Welles, signal *Jersey*, 'Captain repair ashore'," Donland instructed David.

"Aye, Captain," David answered and opened the locker to retrieve the appropriate flags.

"Shall I send a watering party across?" Brunson asked Donland.

"Aye, and send Mister Leeland along to secure any available fresh vegetables, though I can't imagine what might be grown amongst these rocks," Donland answered.

"Aye, Captain," Brunson answered.

Honest followed Donland over the side and down to the boat. "Cold as a witch's tit," Honest said as he seated himself in the boat.

"Aye, as cold as that, let us hope our stay here is short," Donland said.

"Aye," Honest agreed as he tugged his coat tighter.

"Give way all!" Donland ordered the crew.

Three small vessels were anchored close in to the quay. Donland identified two as being fishermen and the third as a small armed ketch. No one was about the deck on any of the vessels. Donland thought it odd, but in this climate of constant wind and blowing rain, being below deck was preferable.

A side party met them at the stone quay. There was the usual twitter of pipes and men called to attention. Donland saluted the flag as stepped forward to take a civilian's offered hand.

"Donald Ivy," the man said and added, "I'm secretary to His Lordship the Viscount Granville, who oversees the waling. He awaits us in the hall."

Cunningham's boat banged against the quay.

"Captain Cunningham, *Jersey*'s captain," Donland introduced.

Ivy said, "A pleasure Captain. Let us go up to the hall."

"Aye," Donland answered.

The small settlement of stone and wood huts was surrounded by tents, presumably for the soldiers. The 'hall' was a two-story stone building, the only one in the settlement.

Donland walked beside Ivy to entrance of the house which was guarded by two soldiers. Ivy asked, as they walked, "Were the ships you encountered Spanish or Portuguese?"

"A frigate shadowed us for three days, I believe her to be the *Liberal*, a Portuguese vessel," Donland answered.

"Was she hostile to you?" Ivy asked.

Donland hedged, "There are different levels of hostile, Mister Ivy. Let me just say that I was on my guard. The two vessels *Jersey* encountered as she sought to land the troops fired on her. I do not know whose they were." He then asked, "I assume by those tents that Major Dormer's contingent has arrived?"

"Yes, he arrived about two hours ago. Quite angrily, I must add. He was not pleased with having to land his men so far from the settlement."

"Did he suffer casualties?"

"I believe he reported four men wounded and none killed."

Donland nodded. Dormer was fortunate.

Both sentries snapped to attention as Ivy, Cunningham and Donland approached. One leaned forward and opened the door. Ivy entered first and to Donland's amazement rather than opening into a large hall they stood in a tiny foyer of no more than four feet deep. "Through here," Ivy said as he opened the door. "Viscount Granville had this door constructed because he despises drafts.

The room Ivy led Donland and Cunningham into had two windows, both covered by heavy drapes. A large blue and red roped rug covered the entire floor, and the room was furnished with two sideboards, a wardrobe and four leather upholstered chairs. Viscount Granville, a slender mustached man no more than fifty sat behind a large table covered in papers and ledgers pouring over a document. The man wore a coat, gloves and hat. The fireplace was roaring and to Donland, unaccustomed to such a fire, it was hot as blazes in the room. He removed his hat and bowed slightly. Viscount Granville appeared not to notice Donland and Ivy's presence.

"He's near deaf!" Ivy whispered.

Ivy announced in a loud voice, "Captain Donland of the *Oxford* and Captain Cunningham of the *Jersey*!"

Granville laid the document down and looked up. He then stroked his mustache as he took in Donland and Cunningham. He nodded and said, "You took your time to report. I prefer my employees to be punctual, is that not correct Ivy?"

Ivy merely answered, "Yes, that is so, your Lordship."

"Have you letters for me or have you forgotten to bring them. I'm sure my partners in London have matters for me to consider and I'll not be delayed in my response," Granville said angrily.

"Your Lordship, would it not be fitting to offer the Captains some refreshment after their long and arduous voyage? We have a fine claret I think you will enjoy and such is only fitting for such a valiant hero of the fleet such as Captain Donland," Ivy said and moved in the direction of the sideboard.

"Quite right, quite right, a claret would not come amiss, a bit to warm the bones." Granville said and rose from his chair.

Donland stood, fighting not to show any emotion. Cunningham turned away and seemed to snicker. Granville was clearly a sick man, perhaps not physically but in other respects. Donland was tempted to open the satchel containing the dispatches but decided it would be best to wait until Granville settled back into his chair.

The only sound in the room was the crackling of the fire while Ivy poured from the crystal decanter. He then turned and offered the goblet to Granville, who promptly lifted it to his lips and drained it. Ivy watched and then took the goblet. He said, "Shall you have claret, my Lord?"

"Yes, yes, I believe so," Granville answered and watched as Ivy refilled the goblet.

Ivy handed Granville the goblet and said, "I will show the officers out."

Granville said nothing and hoisted the goblet to his lips.

Ivy crossed to Donland and took him by the elbow. Donland needed no words of encouragement. He allowed himself to be lead to the door. "If you please, Captain Donland, leave the dispatches with one of the sentries and I shall collect them once I have his lordship settled," Granville whispered as he opened the door.

Donland was mystified. He stood in the small foyer trying to make sense of what just transpired. Shaking his head as if to clear cobwebs, he opened the satchel and pulled out the three oil-cloth wrapped parcels intended for Granville. Then he opened the door stood still for a moment and said to the sentry on his right, "Mister Ivy said he would come to you shortly and collect these."

The sentry eyed the dispatches and then met Donland's eyes, "Not the first time Sir, these will be safe enough until Mister Ivy fetches them."

Donland handed over the dispatches.

Honest rose from the large stone he had sitting on and smiled a knowing smile. After several steps from the sentries he said, "Bit of a cuckoo, was he?"

Donland chuckled and said, "Let us return to our ships."

"Aye," Cunningham replied. "I'd not expected that."

"Nor, I," Donland agreed.

A young army ensign was loitering at the quay. He approached Donland and Honest. "Beg pardon, Captain Donland, I've come from Major Dormer. He requests you attend him before returning to your ship."

Donland was taken aback. He asked, "Are you privy to the reason he requests my attending him?"

"Sir, I am not but he instructed me to approach you only after you had met with Lord Granville," The young ensign stated.

"Well very, I will attend him before returning to *Oxford*. Lead the way, if you please," Donland said.

The ensign replied, "This way, Sir, it is the house just yonder."

Donland and Honest followed after the ensign to the large single floor house built of gray stone. Two sentries flanked the door, and both came to attention as the ensign approached.

The door opened into a large hall with three doors to each side. The only furnishings in the hall were two benches, one on either side of the hall. The ensign knocked at the first door to the right.

"Enter!" Dormer's voice commanded.

"You best wait here," the ensign said to Honest.

"Aye," Honest agreed and turned to sit on the nearby bench.

Donland followed the ensign into the room, which he reasoned was the headquarters. It contained regimental flags on poles in one corner. Dormer was standing behind a large table covered in maps, ledgers and documents. Standing behind a smaller table, also covered in ledgers and documents, was Lieutenant George.

"Good of you to attend me, Captain Donland," Dormer said as he came from behind the table to shake hands.

"I must say that I was a little taken aback by the request but when your ensign said I was to do so after seeing his lordships, I understood the request.

"Aye, yes," Dormer said as he released Donland's hand. "I've Madeira if you would care for a glass?"

"Thank you but no," Donland answered.

"Then let us get to the matter, sit if you will," Dormer said indicating a nearby chair.

"Aye," Donland answered and sat. He waited for Dormer to do likewise.

"Lord Granville is not a well man, I believe you discovered that for yourself," Dormer began. "My orders are to ascertain the situation here. I shall be meeting with the Dons to see if there might be some means of re-establishing Port Egmont and if not then my men and I will await your return. Granville is to return to England as expeditiously as possible and that means aboard your vessel. A letter has been sent to Ivy, his secretary is to accompany Lord Granville. You are to remain at anchor until Ivy has set matters in order. I would, if I could, give you some idea how long that will require, but I cannot. Do you anticipate difficulties by remaining at anchor for a few days?"

Donland was again taken aback; he anticipated having passengers, but not a lord. "I would think not, *Oxford* has stores enough for several weeks. Once I have replenished our water, I will be ready to sail, but I need not if required to linger here two or more days." Donland answered.

"Excellent," Dormer said.

At this point Donland wasn't quite sure how he should address Dormer. He hedged and asked, "Major, will there be others to be transported?"

"Yes, there will be eight others. Six soldiers will be returning to England and I'm told there are two civilians that I've not met."

"Then I will instruct Captain Cunningham to arrange accommodations for Lord Granville and the others aboard *Jersey.*"

"That is entirely your decision. My orders are merely to arrange their transport. Though, I would add that Lord Granville might be difficult. I've had two meetings with him and neither was satisfactory. His secretary, Ivy, will have a difficult time of it."

"Aye," Donland agreed with a half-smile.

The air hung heavy between them for a few moments. Dormer said, "I think you now understand my desire for taking action against that ship that sought to interfere. I could not tell you at the time of my new responsibilities, for I was not certain of what they would be. My instructions stated that I was to use my judgment as to what was to be done with his Lordship. I trust you could see my dilemma?"

Donland replied, "Aye, you were placed in an awkward situation. And, I assume that you were warned prior to our leaving that there might be interference such as we encountered."

"I was," Dormer admitted. "I will also tell you that my reports will bear out my admiration for your discernment of the situation and your skill at avoiding an international incident that may well have lead to greater conflict."

Donland said, "This is such a small corner of the world, I do not understand why any nation would risk war over these rocks."

"Nor do I," Dormer said. "But, my understanding is that whaling is highly profitable and whales are in abundance around these islands. The money men, such as Granville, have the King's ear and see profit even in such remote places as this."

"Aye, fortunes to be made or lost always put soldiers and sailors in harm's way," Donland stated.

"That, Captain Donland sums it up quite nicely."

Donland dined that evening with Captain Cunningham aboard the *Jersey*. The meal was plain fare consisting of boiled beef, cabbage and fresh baked bread brought from the island.

Cunningham said after the meal, "Fancy food is a waste of hard-earned money. And for the likes of me, money saved for my old age. In my time I've seen so many captains of vessels like *Jersey* cast ashore that if I do not prepare, me and mine will go hungry. Their Lordships in the Admiralty cast us off as easily as a woman does her ragged flock for a new one. I tell you sir, I'll not go hungry."

"Aye, a man who doesn't prepare is a fool," Donland said. He then asked, "How long have you served *Jersey*?"

The man grinned and said, "You do not know the story of how I obtained her?"

Donland truthfully answered, "No, I've not heard."

Cunningham grinned, showing a yellowed set of almost perfect teeth. He then said, "From second lieutenant to command. Quite a step for one so young, much like your own tale." He paused and drank a large sip of wine. "As I said, I was second, been aboard four years and should have been first after two but Captain Archibald Bainbridge would not have me for it. He chose his second cousin named Elkins, who knew no more about sailing than a cat knows about how to catch a fox. Anyway, we were off the Dutch Slave Coast having just transported a company of Royal Guards when a flock of them black buggers in their little boats boarded us one moonless night.

We fought, captain Bainbridge was killed as was Elkins. Me and about a dozen others stood our ground on the foredeck and fought em' off. When the sun came up, we was half a crew. Youngster by the name of Churchill, newly come aboard to the midshipman's berth, wrote the whole affair down in a letter. Wasn't until we dropped our anchor and I reported to the admiralty that I knew anything about it. Turned out that Churchill was related to some nob in the Admiralty and that was who received the lad's letter. For my heroism, I got *Jersey*, been aboard her fourteen years and captain for ten."

"I commend you Captain, you more than earned your step," Donland said.

"Aye, I earned it, but there are those who fault me for the loss of Bainbridge and have sentenced me to this fate. Captain of a cow of a vessel," Cunningham said. He lifted his glass and drank. Setting down the glass he said, "I stopped complaining when so many were cast up on the beach. I've a good berth."

"Aye, as do I," Donland said.

Cunningham changed tack and asked, "Are we to go back empty?"

"I'm told you will have less than a dozen to transport."

"Sick and infirmed?" Cunningham asked.

Donland sipped wine and answered, "Some to some degree."

"Honesty, if you please Isaac," Cunningham said using Donland's given name.

Donland blew a breath. He decided now was as good a time as any to pass on the bad news. "Lord Granville will be returning to England. Accompanying him will be his secretary, Mister Ivy."

Cunningham frowned and said, "I do not fair well with nobs."

"I would rather not be the one to bear bad news but I must," Donland said. He continued, "You asked if those sailing with you would be sick and infirmed, I answered truthfully and said yes. You saw and heard with your own ears his condition. It is for that reason that he is returning home."

Cunningham erupted, "Blast them all to hell and back! I'm to contend with a crazy man and him a nob!"

Donland sought to soothe Cunningham's temper, "Mister Ivy will mind him, he should be no trouble to you and you'll not have to entertain him."

"Is that your supposition, Sir, or do you know this to be a fact?" Cunningham asked.

"You've met with Lord Granville and witnessed how Ivy attended him," Donland said, fearing to say more.

"From what you say and the way you said it, I take it that the man Ivy has the make of Lord Granville?"

"Aye," Donland said and added, "I'll say no more of the man."

"Then I shall not either. When do we sail?" Cunningham asked.

Donland was pleased to change the topic of conversation. "Two or three days, Major Dormer is the acting governor and he shall instruct me," Donland answered.

Chapter Five

"Shall I send some of the men ashore?" Powell asked as Donland wrote in the ledger.

"Aye, as you determine prudent," Donland said without looking up.

"I was considering sending two dozen accompanied by one midshipman and one lieutenant as there are a number of soldiers about and there might be trouble in the pubs."

Donland looked up and said with some exasperation, "As you will Mister Powell, as you will!"

"Aye, Captain," Powell answered with sharpness. He then turned and left the office.

As soon as the door closed, Donland heard a commotion. He started to rise but Powell's voice shouted, "Announce him!"

"Not necessary!" a voice answered and the door immediately opened, Donland was about to scold Powell but then froze. The figure in the door wore a long brown boat-cloak and a floppy hat.

"My fault Captain!" the young marine sentry said as he pushed past the man. He then attempted to push the intruder back out of the door.

"Belay!" Donland shouted.

The marine looked puzzled.

"You are dismissed Gilchrist, return to your post," Donland said as he rose from the chair.

"Captain Donland, beg pardon for the intrusion," the man said followed by a wide grin.

"Captain!" Honest said as he burst through the side door with his knife at the ready. Seeing the man in the boat-cloak he exclaimed, "Damn my eyes!"

The man said nothing but fished a cheroot case from his pocket. No one spoke as he lit the foul-smelling tobacco. He puffed and said, "It is good to see you too."

Donland responded as Honest moved beside the desk, "I've seen many a sight but none as surprising as seeing you burst through my door. What in the King's name are you doing here, Mathis?"

"You are correct in your assertion, in the king's name. I'm here at the behest of King George and those who have authority over you. I'm to sail with you to Antigua, I trust that will be to your liking," Mathis Sumerford stated.

It took effort, but Donland attempted not to show his amazement. "You then are one of the two civilians to be transported?"

"Preferable aboard this vessel," Sumerford stated and then sat in the chair in front of Donland's desk.

"Of course," Donland said and then asked, "What are you doing here?"

Sumerford blew a cloud of blue smoke. "As I said; service to the king. Other than that, I cannot say, but perhaps over the next few days you might pry a bit more from me. A good brandy has a way of loosening my tongue."

"I've other ways to loosen your tongue," Honest interjected.

"I'm sure you do," Sumerford said. "On others but not on me for my secrets go to the grave if need be."

"Then so be it," Honest said and slapped a fist into his palm.

"Fetch me something to drink, if you will Honest, something to wash away the salt," Sumerford toyed.

"Aye," Donland said. "Three glasses, if you please, Honest."

"Aye," Honest answered and grinned.

Donland resumed his seat. He stared across the desk and asked, "On the king's business, you say, have you given up your new country?"

"I've not, but as my new country has been called upon to assist my old country my services were sought."

"A spy is always a spy," Donland quipped.

"And a peacemaker is always a peacemaker," Sumerford retorted.

"How so?" Donland asked as he received a glass from Honest.

"That, I am not at liberty to disclose. Suffice it to say my task was accomplished successfully. I can file my reports to both parties who have sought my talents with satisfaction."

"And receive more than a king's ransom in payment," Honest said.

Sumerford laughed, then accepted the glass Honest offered. He took a sip and said, "Not as much as that but sufficient to cover my expenditures."

"How long have you been here?" Donland asked.

"Six weeks, I was transported on a rather fragile craft with a cantankerous oaf of a master."

"Jackson?" Donland asked.

"Yes, I believe that to be his name. A bit wheezy but sober-minded, knew his stuff."

Donland laughed and said, "Aye, a good sailor and navigator."

"I tried to engage him to remain while I pursued my task but he complained of the weather and his aching bones. He left me here to manage my own passage. Your arrival is most fortunate."

"Some may call me a fool but your knowledge of me prevents you from doing so, does it not?" Donland asked.

"That is so, and yes I knew you were providing transport for Major Dormer's troops. Therefore, my transport from this place was assured." Sumerford drank and said, "Major Dormer asked me to inform you that you may sail tomorrow."

"You are eager to be away?" Donland asked.

"As I said, I've reports to make and the information I bear is urgent, so yes, I prefer to be away as soon as possible."

"I will have to consult with Captain Cunningham of the *Jersey* about sailing arrangements. I'm tasked with the protection of the transport."

"The captain has been notified," Sumerford said, cutting Donland off. He added, "He is to make his own way and you are to convey me to Antigua with all haste."

"You have orders to that effect?" Donland asked.

"I have the authority and the orders are mine to make. Do you care to read my authorization?

Donland half-smiled and said, "Were I still a mere lieutenant in command of a sloop I would have said no. But, as a post captain and command His Majesty's *Oxford*, I must insist on seeing proper authorization. You do understand?"

Sumerford grinned and reached into his pocket, pulled out a leather wallet and extracted a small folded piece of parchment. He carefully unfolded the document, then handed it across.

Donland glanced at it, noted the signature. It was signed by Prime Minister William Pitt. He said as he handed the document back to Sumerford, "If the signature is valid then you do indeed have the authority. I cannot verify it so on the basis of my trust in you and your word, *Oxford* is at your disposal."

"As she should be," Sumerford said as he placed the document back into his wallet. "Now that you are satisfied, you may begin your preparations."

"Aye," Donland answered. He turned to Honest, "My compliments to Lieutenant Powell, he is to belay sending men ashore."

"Aye, Captain," Honest answered and went straightway to the door.

"A good fellow," Sumerford said.

"Aye, that he is and loyal,"

Sumerford dropped his cheroot to the deck and squashed it with his boot. "As are you, unlike some I could name which is why I was chosen for my current task. You may have doubts about me but I can assure you that my intentions and actions are honorable for both your king and my president. I look forward, over the coming days, of engaging you in conversation. I have knowledge of events and also speculations of events that you will find intriguing and perhaps beneficial to you."

"Secrets?" Donland asked.

Sumerford grinned and answered firmly, "No!"

The door opened and Powell entered, followed by Honest.

"Mister Powell, are all our people aboard?" Donland asked as Powell removed his hat.

"Aye, Captain except for Mister Leeland and the boat crew The others Honest stopped from going ashore just as the boat was about to set off."

"Very good, send Mister Welles ashore to fetch the purser. We will weigh anchor at first light."

"Aye, Captain," Powell said and then asked, "Are we to shepherd *Jersey*?"

"No, Captain Cunningham will be on his own. We will be sailing for Antigua with as much dash as we can manage."

Powell grinned and said, "Dash will hardly describe our ability."

"Ability or no, it will be with all the haste we can muster," Donland said.

Powell could not help but to add, "To rid ourselves of an irritation."

"If you mean, Mister Sumerford, then yes. We are ordered to deliver him."

"As I thought," Powell said. "I shall fetch Mister Welles."

Donland turned his attention to Sumerford. "Tell me truthfully, Mathias, will there be those opposing your return?"

Mathias glanced up to the skylight and held a finger to his nose. "Mister Powell indicated that the wind will be opposing us, is that true?"

"Aye, it is so; we shall be crisscrossing the wind to make headway until we escape the westerlies. Once nearer the equator the winds will turn favorable. You did not answer my question."

Again, Sumerford put a finger to his nose and said, "Opposing winds will greatly reduce sailing speed. I should think you would prepare for them."

Donland understood. Sumerford was using the wind to say that there are those who may attack *Oxford* to keep her from reaching Antigua. "Then I shall have extra hands aloft and on deck should an emergency arise."

Sumerford smiled and said, "Then I shall sleep soundly knowing you have a clear understanding of the peril opposing winds may bring."

"As to sleeping, Rowland, inform Mister Brunson that he will be sharing Mister Andrews' cabin. Arrange to have Mister Sumerford's dunnage placed in the cabin," Donland ordered.

"Aye, Captain," Rowland replied.

Sumerford rose. "I'm sure you have affairs to arrange and I have some letters and a report to write."

"Will you dine with me tonight?" Donland asked.

"As you wish, Isaac, as you wish," Sumerford answered.

Donland called to him before he reached the door, "I have a new cook, and she is very skilled."

"Indeed, I shall look forward to the meal. Will Mister Powell and Mister Welles be joining us?"

"As you wish," Donland replied mocking him.

Rosita prepared lobsters, steamed carrots with onions and a platter of crispy fried potatoes. Rowland helped with the serving while Honest dined alone in the galley.

51

"My word, a meal fit for the king himself," Sumerford said after the platters were placed on the table.

"Aye, and will be as delicious as any Frenchman could desire," Donland stated with a hint of pride.

"There will be rice pudding afterwards," Rosita said with a smile.

David was delighted and exclaimed, "My favorite!"

Sumerford cracked his lobster with a small wooden mallet. He scooped a forkful of white meat from the tail and popped it into his mouth. He chewed and said before swallowing, "Magnificent!"

The only conversation as the men ate was to ask for more wine. David, used to the fare in the midshipmen's berth, was the first to finish. Donland smiled, thinking back to his own days of the midshipmen's berth. He was never invited to his captain's table.

Sumerford sipped wine; his plate was empty except for the lobster carcass. "I've not enjoyed such a fine meal since I was last in New Orleans."

"And when was that?" Powell inquired.

"Just over five months ago, that is where I was when I was summoned back to Charleston," Sumerford said.

"Is that where you encountered Mister Jackson and *Folly*?" Donland asked.

"Yes it was, I was in need of transport and he was unloading his cargo. Wasn't pleased to see be nor open to my request for passage."

"Pound notes persuaded him and I would image quite a few of them," Powell interjected.

Sumerford leaned back in his chair. "He refused the king's coin said any sensible man would accept only gold American dollars. So, we struck a bargain, a costly one I might add."

Donland pushed his plate aside and said, "I can only imagine."

Rosita entered bearing a tray with dishes of rice pudding. Sumerford asked her, "Have you a husband, dear lady?"

"Si," Rosita said and added, "He is below and he kill you!"

Sumerford's face registered shock, and then he laughed.

"It is true," Donland said. "She is married, and he is below on the gun-deck and he will kill you if I fail to do so!"

They all laughed.

The evening wound down with David departing for his hammock and Powell to the deck. Sumerford said as David closed the door, "You've not asked about Betty?"

Donland smiled and replied, "No, I've not because I received a letter two months ago. You said that you left Charleston well before her letter was written and arrived to me. She said that she was in Boston and I therefore concluded that you've no communication with her."

Sumerford pulled his case from his coat as Donland was speaking. He extracted a cheroot and lit it. After a puff he said, "And how is the lady?"

"Well and she did say that you had been to her home and departed for New Orleans."

"All that is true, did she say that she pines for you every day?"

Donland laughed. "No she did not, only that she misses me," he said.

"It was what she said to me," Sumerford said and blew smoke.

The cheroot's foul smell filled the cabin. It was the third one Sumerford had lit since the meal ended.

"Have you a chest of those?" Donland asked.

Sumerford laughed and replied, "Yes I do, seems that I no sooner finish one than I desire another. I frequently run out of matches."

"Shall we go on deck?" Donland asked.

"You find my smoking offensive?" Sumerford asked.

Donland replied, "Aye, the smell of it."

"Then let us go out on deck and stand in the rain like two fools," Sumerford said as he stood.

Chapter Six

Oxford weighted her anchors at first light. The sky was a slate gray and rain pelted all those on deck. They were no sooner out of the channel when Bill called down from the masthead, "Deck there! Sail!" He pointed in the direction.

Donland took a glass from the rack; there was no mistaking the Portuguese frigate.

"Three sail!" Bill shouted down

"No doubt the two sloops that fired on *Jersey*," Powell said.

"Aye, Donland agreed.

"Shall we go to quarters?" Powell asked.

Oxford crashed into her first heavy roller. "Not as yet, we'll not give him the pleasure of thinking he has unsettled us," Donland answered.

They stood there in the rain watching the frigate and sloops rising and falling on the rollers. Winslow advised sailing due east for half a day to gain more favorable winds at the edge of the westerlies. Donland agreed even though sailing into the teeth of such waves was not appealing.

"We will maintain course, set all sail, if you please Mister Powell," Donland said.

He put the glass to his eye again. The frigate was adjusting her yards to either intercept *Oxford* or to shadow her. If there were to be an attack, it would come when the wind was favorable and the sloops were in position to render support. Sumerford interrupted his thoughts.

"Do you recognize them?"

"Aye, Portuguese," Donland answered without turning.

"I'm not surprised," Sumerford said. "I believe she is the same one that chased *Folly*. Jackson, that crafty devil, managed to slip away from her one very dark night."

"And that's why you wanted him rather than another," Donland said and grinned. "He's crafty!"

"That he is, almost but not quite your match," Sumerford said.

"Mister Powell, pass the word for Mister Andrews to come aft. Mister Hornsby will assume his duties at the foremast."

"Aye, Captain," Powell answered.

Sumerford asked, "You have something in mind?"

"Aye and you will know when Mister Andrews knows," Donland replied smugly.

Sumerford gave a short laugh and said, "And you will know my plans when I tell you."

Donland did not reply. He watched as Andrews hurried along the deck dodging between working hands and deck equipment. He then lifted the glass to his eye. The two sloops were clearer, no more than a mile and a half distant. The frigate was less than a mile and converging.

Donland lowered the glass. Andrews saluted.

"Mister Andrews go below prepare one of the transom guns. I would like to persuade our shadow to keep his distance. A warning only, is that clear?"

Andrews smiled and said, "Aye Captain, a warning only. Extra power for more smoke."

"Do not fire until I send word and do not load again but stand by the gun until you are recalled."

"Aye Captain," Andrews answered and asked, "Is that all, Sir?"

Donland half-smiled and said, "It is Mister Andrews, see to your task."

"Aye Captain," Andrews said and turned from the quarterdeck.

Sumerford said to Donland's back, "A prudent decision, Captain Donland."

Donland ignored the remark and called, "Mister Powell, We will go about! Starboard tack once around!"

"Aye Captain," Powell answered from the waist.

"Stand by to go about!" Powell shouted into his trumpet.

Instantly the call was relayed up and down the deck. Men raced to their stations while laggards felt the sting of the bo'sun's rattan.

Satisfied all were on station and the braces manned, Powell turned to the quarterdeck.

"Now, if you please Mister Powell," Donland ordered.

Winslow called aloud, "Ready ho!"

"Aye," the helmsmen answered in unison.

"Helm a'lee!" Winslow shouted.

The shout carried along the deck and Hornsby in command of the foremast shouted, "Headsail sheets let go!"

As the other sails were hauled round the hands bent to the tasks. Blocks banged and sails flapped as *Oxford* changed direction. The men at the braces leaned their weight into hauling the great yards round until they filled and were pressed hard by the wind. *Oxford* heeled and dove into the rollers.

Donland maintain vigilance on the frigate and the two sloops. The frigate and her consorts did exactly as he expected and attempted to match *Oxford*'s maneuver.

"Mister Vickers, my compliments to Mister Andrews, he is to fire one round!"

"Aye, Captain, one round!" Simon answered and hurried to go below.

Powell was busy bringing order back to the deck after having to go-about. He and the other lieutenants were shouting and cajoling men to, "Clean up that rabble! Set that to rights! You there, jump to it!"

The frigate was just over a half-mile off *Oxford*'s aft quarter. Andrews fired. The boom of the gun took many aboard by surprise but not Donland.

"That should give them pause," Sumerford said to Donland's back.

"Aye, and if it did not, he'll have another to consider. I mean for him and his pack to keep their distance," Donland said as he faced Sumerford.

"Should he?" Sumerford asked.

Donland grinned and said, "He will for he knows our reach is longer than his and we have more weight of metal. He may have speed and agility but it will only get him so close before receiving severe damage."

"I see your point," Sumerford said.

Donland turned and studied the frigate. She had changed her course several degrees and appeared to have reduced sail. He knew his tactics were only a temporary measure for if the frigate captain was bent on taking *Oxford*, doing so would only take place when opportunity presented itself and favored the frigate and cohorts.

"Hold this course as long as possible, Mister Winslow. We'll go about and tack to larboard within the hour. I hope to reach favorable wind before nightfall."

"Aye, Captain, we should," Winslow said.

"Mister Sumerford, there are matters I wish to discuss with you, please join me in my cabin," Donland said.

Sumerford replied, "Perhaps it is time," and followed Donland from the quarterdeck.

The office had no skylight and with the door closed there was little danger of being overheard. He closed the door after Sumerford; he did not sit. He began, "I will not inquire into what our masters have tasked you to be about but I must know about the risks I am undertaking."

Sumerford nodded and said, "My intention was to tell you once we were away. You are correct in that now is the time to explain our difficulties. I was sent as an American citizen to ascertain what if any alliances were being made between France and other nations in this hemisphere. Also, I was evaluating what naval forces may be brought to bear if those alliances were made. And thirdly, I was to judge the danger to our whaling interests. You may not appreciate the fact that a third of all the crown's whale oil comes from The Falklands. Your friend, Jackson, and his little ship were the perfect cover for my tasks. He is, as I stated a crafty fellow and was well suited for the task. I could not risk capture on my return so I waited for your arrival."

He was interrupted by a knock at the door.

"Come!" Donland said.

Rowland entered and asked, "Captain do you require refreshments?"

"No, I do not!" Donland snapped and added, "Go forward to the bowsprit and stay there until I send for you!"

Rowland's face reflected his puzzlement. He replied, "Aye, Captain," and closed the door.

"He heard?" Sumerford asked.

"Probably but he will not speak a word no matter who attempts to pry it from him," Donland said. He stared hard at Sumerford and asked, "What have you not told me?"

Sumerford grinned then rubbed his chin, "Very well, have you heard of a man named Raymond de Sèze?"

"No, I assume it is French?"

"He is and is a man I've opposed before. He, like me, is one who manages to stay in the shadows of events."

"A spy," Donland interjected.

"And more, he's a man who has the ear of the powerful and is able persuade such people. I dare say that his cunning is unmatched by any man I've known and that makes him very dangerous. He is the reason I am aboard your ship."

"You came across him in your recent travels?" Donland asked.

Sumerford nodded and said, "I did indeed to my surprise. He was in the port of Rio de Janeiro in talks with Portuguese nobles. My understanding was that he arrived aboard the French vessel *Viala*, a seventy-four."

Donland said, "I'd not want to oppose her with *Oxford*."

"To my knowledge she has remained at anchor in Rio de Janeiro but I do believe De Sèze sent that frigate to prevent me from reporting what I've uncovered. He assumed in-correctly that I boarded your ship en route to the islands, and that is why you were chased."

Donland rubbed his chin thoughtfully. He sighed and said, "If De Sèze is what you have said then the captain of that frigate will risk all to accomplish his task."

"That is the danger you face," Sumerford said.

"Aye," Donland agreed. "He will bide his time until he senses a weakness and come at us like a hungry wolf. I do not doubt that his orders are to destroy us and leave no trace."

"That would be what I would order and as I said, De Sèze is cunning and ruthless," Sumerford said.

Donland returned to the deck and checked the position of the frigate. She was three-quarters of a mile distant. The two sloops were with-in hailing distance of her.

"Planning an attack?" Powell asked.

"Aye perhaps, but I would wager that Captain Capral is laying a plan for another day. He means to take us, of that I'm certain," Donland answered.

Powell studied Donland's face and asked, "Do you know why?"

"Yes but I'll not discuss it here. I will confide in you later, rest assured of that. For now, however, we will see to our duties," Donland said.

He turned to Winslow and asked, "Mister Winslow what of the wind?"

"It'll hold Captain, no change. Blasted rain as well," Winslow answered.

"We will go about onto a larboard tack, Mister Powell," Donland said with resolve.

"Aye, Captain, and the next tack will be to starboard?"

"We have to make use of the wind we have. I will leave the ship handling to you," Donland answered.

"Mister Vickers," Donland addressed the youngster. "My compliments to Mister Andrews, he is to report to me."

"Aye, Captain," Simon answered.

Donland smiled as he observed the frigate begin her preparations to go about as her captain saw *Oxford*'s sails begin to shift. It would be this way for the rest of the day.

Six bells rang out loud and clear as Winslow shouted, "Helm a' lee!"

"Beg pardon, captain," Andrews said to Donland's back.

Donland turned, "Aye, Mister Andrews, have you a good crew on that gun?"

"Aye, Sir," Andrews replied.

"Good, they will gain a good deal of practice this day. We will be beating back and forth until we find favorable wind. I want you to fire at that frigate whenever you judge her to be within a mile of *Oxford*. Hit her if you can!"

Andrews grinned and said, "Aye, Captain!"

Oxford came onto her new course. The frigate did likewise maintaining her three-quarter mile distance. The sky overheard remained an unbroken thick cloud with steady soaking rain. Donland wasn't concerned about their true course. *Oxford* was barely making two knots and with the drift it was impossible to calculate her true course. *Oxford*'s course-made-good would only be corrected when she reached the trades and found a clear sky.

"I doubt we will have sun for the noon-day sighting," Donland said to Winslow.

"Perhaps tomorrow," Winslow said and added, "We've sea-room for any maneuver."

"Aye," Donland answer and tugged his boat-cloak tight around his neck.

Andrews' gun boomed reminding everyone of the threat Donland perceived. None would know the reason for keeping the frigate at bay and would speculate wildly. They knew, to a man, that war had not been declared and that firing on any vessel violated the laws of the sea. Even though they did not know the why of it, they would not question Donland's judgment or his orders.

Noon came and went as did the dog-watch. At each tack, the frigate and the two sloops matched *Oxford*'s. Powell expressed his frustration by saying, "I would that he get on with it!" Donland did not reply even though he had the same thought.

"Mister Powell, pass the word that there will be no lights on deck, or the gundecks," Donland ordered as he left the quarterdeck.

"The binnacle?" Powell asked.

"Only that!" Donland answered over his shoulder.

Rowland was waiting with a dry shirt and breeches in the state room. Donland gladly pulled off his wet uniform and donned the dry clothes. Roland then handed Donland a hot mug.

"What is it Donland asked after taking a sip?" He had expected coffee but it something entirely different.

"Rosita called it cocoa, Sir. I've never tasted the like before," Roland answered.

Donland took another sip and found it to be very sweet, smooth and not bitter like coffee or tea.

"What is it made from?" Donland asked.

"Some kind of pod, bigger than coffee beans," Rowland said and added, "She ground it into a power."

Rain continued to beat against the quarter window glass. Donland turned toward the window and observed that the night was falling quickly. He strained to see the frigate as he sipped the cocoa. She showed no lights, it was as he thought. He tried to put himself into the frigate captain's mind. "What would he do?"

There was a knock at the outer door. "Enter!" he shouted.

"Beg pardon, Captain, Mister Andrews compliments Sir, he sent me," Midshipman Mellencamp said.

"What is it, Mister Mellencamp?" The boy was physically shaking. His hat and coat was sodden through and through as were his stockings and shoes.

"Mister Andrews has secured the gun for the night. He asks if he is to man the gun at first light."

Donland considered the question; Andrews would have the watch, Malcolm would not. He answered, "Tell him no, pass the word for Mister Malcolm to report to me."

"Aye, Captain," Mellencamp said and started to turn for the door.

Donland ordered, "Belay Mister Mellencamp." The boy stopped, his face was already white with chill. His eyes filled with fear as he stood still.

"Rowland," Donland called.

The steward appeared at once from behind the curtain. "Captain?"

"Is there more cocoa?" Donland asked.

"Aye, Sir."

"Let us see what the youngster thinks of it. Fetch him a cup."

"Aye, Captain," Rowland said and his face lit into a broad smile.

Donland said, "I've something hot to drink before you seek out Mister Andrews."

Rowland came from behind the curtain bearing a mug of cocoa and handed it to Mellencamp who took it, looked at

Donland and said, "Thank you, Captain." He peered into the cup then brought it to his lips and sipped.

Donland watched as the boy's eyes widened in surprise. "How is it?" He asked.

"Delicious, Sir!" Mellencamp said and lifted the cup again.

Donland smiled and said, "Finish it in the dining room, Mister Mellencamp. When you've finished, my compliments to both Mister Andrews and Mister Malcolm."

"Aye, Captain," the boy answered with a smile and a half-moon of coca on his upper lip.

Donland smiled as a memory of a kindness was shown to him once when he was a midshipman by his first lieutenant. It was the first of the few acts of kindness shown him. Such acts were treasured and remembered as he hoped Mellencamp would do.

A tapping at the door signaled one or both of the lieutenants were reporting.

"Enter!" Donland said and rose from the dining chair.

The door opened and Andrews entered followed by Malcolm, both with hats tucked under their arms and dripping water.

"Mister Andrews your performance with the gun this afternoon was admirable. However, as you have the morning watch, Mister Malcolm will take up your duties with the gun when the light returns," Donland ordered.

"Aye, Captain," both men said together.

Chapter Seven

An hour later, Donland paused, the logbook open before him. He determined that something was different and rose from his chair and entered the main cabin and crossed to the side galley. The rain had stopped.

There was an urgent knocking at the door.

"Enter!" He called.

"Beg pardon, Captain, Mister Powell asks that you come on deck. The wind has changed," David said.

"I'll come," Donland answered.

Rowland appeared with a dry coat and hat. Donland slipped on the coat and clamped the hat on his head.

The first thing he did after gaining the quarterdeck was to look up, checking the set of sails. Here and there in the black sky, stars twinkled.

Powell said to him, "Mister Winslow says that we've not reached the trades and that this wind will not hold for long."

"I'll not complain," Donland said. He turned to starboard and asked, "What of our shadow?"

"No lights," Powell said. "I suspect he is still there."

"Aye, and with the change of wind I'll wager he is not content to be the shadow any longer. Call all hands, if you please, quietly! We will go about and confuse the bugger! South by West!"

"Aye, Captain! He'll not expect that," Powell answered.

"Nor should he, Mister Powell, nor should he!"

Donland remained on deck as *Oxford* came round and settled on the course from which she had come. "Hold this course for one hour, no more then we will lie-to for the night. Mister Powell, Instruct the men that I want to noise, no singing, no fiddles and certainly no whistles!"

"Aye, Captain," Powell answered. He hesitated a moment then asked, "Are we not to fight?"

Donland replied, "No, Mister Powell." He then turned away and made for his cabin. Honest followed on his heels.

Rowland met Donland in the dining room and helped remove his coat and took his hat. Honest waited then asked, "Is it a wise decision?"

Donland turned on him and said, "It is my decision and I'll thank you not to inquire further. Rig some sailcloth over the transom windows and pass the word for Mister Winslow to join me in the chart room."

"Aye," Honest answered.

Winslow pushed open the door to the chart room and closed it behind him. In his hand he was holding a rolled chart. "You sent for me Captain?"

"Aye, Mister Winslow. I make our position to be about here. How much am I off?" Donland held his finger over the spot.

Winslow leaned over the chart, rubbed his chin and said, "Closer to here, Sir, nearer 50.1 degrees north by 57.0 east," Winslow said and indicated the position.

"What of the wind?" Donland asked.

"Hard to say Captain, I've not sailed this sea afore, I have only my charts," Winslow stated. "But, the charts do indicate that if we continue nor' east we will reach the trades. Though I've noticed the barometer falling, could be a gale to come."

"Let us pray not," Donland said with a grin.

"What of the morning?" Winslow inquired.

Donland considered the question; he put his finger on the chart. There was nothing but open sea for hundreds of miles in all directions. Sumerford had ordered him to Antigua, a voyage of seven weeks. *Oxford* would be low on stores by then, and water would be a precious commodity. And there was the frigate and her consorts to be considered.

"Let us see what wind we have," Donland said in answer to Winslow's question.

"Aye, Captain," Winslow said and asked, "Do you need me further?"

"No Mister Winslow, you may return to your duties. Please pass the word for Mister Powell and Mister Sumerford to join me."

"Aye Captain," Winslow said and sauntered from the chart room.

Donland sighed and turned to study the chart. There was a nagging question in his brain, it had not fully formed. Sumerford had said that he was on a fact-finding mission for the Crown and for the Americans. Whale oil was an important war-time commodity. Information about what vessels might be available to oppose England's navy was also important. But such information, in his mind, was not so vital as to risk a frigate and two sloops or the sinking of *Oxford*. The nagging question had to be that there was something more important at stake. Something Sumerford had not revealed.

Powell arrived first. "Wind has died, and the rain has returned," he said as he shook water from his hat.

"I've coffee," Donland said.

Powell smiled and said, "That would be welcome with a drop or two of rum."

"Rowland!" Donland called.

"Aye, Captain! Be but a moment!" Rowland answered.

The cabin was nearly dark with only a single lantern giving off it's feeble light. Sailcloth covered the transom windows and Powell was barely visible in the gloom. They sat without speaking aware of the creaking, banging and rattles of the ship. He could hear low conversation taking place on the poop deck above him. Moments later there was faint laughter.

Donland asked Powell, "Is the ship dark?"

"Aye," Powell answered just as Rowland entered the cabin bearing two cups on a tray.

"Rowland prepare another cup except without the rum. Mister Sumerford will add his own flavoring when he arrives," Donland ordered.

"Aye, Captain," Rowland answered while handing Powell a cup.

Powell nosily sipped the boiling coffee. Donland did the same.

"Captain," Powell said with hesitancy. "Are we to fight?"

Donland answered by asking, "To what end, James? That frigate captain means not only to take us but also to sink us. War, as far as I know, has not been declared and if he attacks, he can leave no trace. By that same measure, I would have no choice but to sink the frigate and the sloops. It would have to appear they were lost by some other means. Were we to engage there can be no quarter. So, in answer to your question, my intent is to avoid the fight unless there is no means to do so."

Powell spoke softly, "I suppose that is why you've made post and I've not. You see in terms that I've not equipped myself to do so. Were I in command, I'd not hesitate and take all three as prizes. The prize money alone would be enough for me to live as a king."

"Aye, but you'd not receive a penny and land on the beach for having started a war!" Donland said and laughed.

"Aye," Powell agreed and sipped his coffee. He set his cup on the sideboard and asked, "You said you would tell me why the Portuguese are pursuing us, why are they?"

"James, I can truthfully say that the explanation I received is not sufficient to warrant the attack. That being said, Mister Sumerford will have to supply the explanation. He'll not leave this cabin until we have it."

There was a tapping at the outer door, and then it opened. "Deuced dark as a dungeon in here," Sumerford said with a touch of humor.

"Aye," Donland said and added, "I've a coffee for you."

Oxford rocked heavily as a roller passed beneath her hull. In the gloom, Sumerford's foot caught on the leg of a chair. He stumbled forward, banging into a sideboard. "Damn!" he exclaimed. "Surely, a little more light is possible!"

Donland laughed and said, "For a man accustomed to dark ways and methods, I'd think you'd frown on light."

"Your coffee, Sir," Rowland said as he held out a tray with a single cup. He asked, "Shall I add to it?"

"Yes, Scotch would do nicely," Sumerford answered as he made his way to a chair beside Powell.

"Mister Powell, would you also like another cup and rum?" Donland asked.

"I think not Sir; I best maintain a clear head. The night might prove interesting," Powell answered.

"Perhaps so but I am confident it will be uneventful as will the next few days to come," Donland said.

"Will the weather moderate and bring us some sun?" Sumerford asked.

Donland grinned and replied, "If I'm to guess, I would say there will be more rain. It seems endless in the region. We are perhaps a day and a half sailing to the north to reach even what you would call moderate weather. Further south back to The Falklands there will certainly be heavy weather."

"I'd care not to return there again in this lifetime," Powell said.

Sumerford added, "As miserable place on God's earth as there exists."

Donland decided that now was the time to try his ploy. He said, "Aye, that it may be, but we will be returning there at first light. I'll not risk my ship for your report on whale oil."

Sumerford erupted, "You most certainly will not, I've given you my order and I've the backing of the Admiralty. You cannot refuse!"

"I can and I will Mathias. I see no urgency in your reports. My standing orders as Captain of this vessel prevent me from hazarding my command. The Admiralty would not look kindly on starting a war over a report on whale oil or how many ships of a peaceful nation are in their harbors."

Sumerford stood and bellowed, "You are under my orders!"

Powell stood and put a hand on Sumerford's arm. Sumerford shook it off and declared, "Isaac, you have no choice but to obey!"

Donland stood and answered Sumerford, "I am in command of this vessel and my officers will obey my commands. You may carry authority from higher ups, but as long as I command here, it is my word that will be followed. Is that not so Mister Powell?"

"Aye, Captain," Powell answered without hesitation.

Sumerford threatened, "I'll have you on charges!"

Donland countered, "That you may do but only when you reach another station other than the one Major Dormer commands. And as I said, it is my intention to return there unless you can give me a valid reason to proceed toward Antigua."

"My authority is sufficient!" Sumerford countered.

"So you say! But I command!" Donland shouted.

Sumerford made to reach into his pocket. Powell reacted swiftly by shoving Sumerford with enough force that he again fell against the sideboard.

"Enough!" Donland shouted.

The two marine guards burst through the door, their bayoneted muskets at the ready.

"Belay!" Donland shouted to the marines. "Return to your posts!"

The marines looked one to another and without a word turned back for the door.

To Powell, Donland said, "Help him to his feet."

"You'll regret that," Sumerford said, and he shook away Powell's hand. "You'll both regret this night!"

Donland said calmly, "Perhaps, but right now I regret nothing. You are a man of secrets and you hold them to yourself without regard for the well-being of those called upon to assist you. In the past, I have obeyed you without question. We've fought side by side, you've saved my life and I'll always hold you dear for that. But, this night, before I proceed to Antigua or turn back to The Falklands, I need to know the truth of the matter. What is it that puts this ship in harm's way?"

Sumerford shifted himself and tugged at his coat. "Very well, I will tell you, but I'll not forget this incident. You will understand the urgency of my report and I'll require you to proceed with all haste to Antigua. Do you agree?"

"Aye, if I deem the urgency worthy of the risk," Donland answered.

"You will, that I can assure you," Sumerford said. "Have you a chart of the Rio de Janeiro harbor?"

"Mister Powell, if you please bring it from the chart room," Donland said in the way of answering Sumerford.

"Aye," Powell said and started off for the chart.

"The information you are so eager to take to Antigua has to do with ships in that harbor?" Donland asked.

"Not ships in the harbor, ships being built," Sumerford answered.

Donland was taken aback. "The Portuguese are building ships?"

"They and the French, it is a joint effort. One that neither the American navy was aware of or the Admiralty and I confess that it was stumbled on only by accident. A conversation was overheard in Europe, I'll not say where or who heard it. The person bearing the information is of impeccable reputation so when it came to the ears of the Prime Minister, the task fell to me to investigate. My report will contain that information and a plan to respond to the building of those ships. The French, Portuguese and Spanish are not only making allies in South America but also they have a plan to push the British out of these waters and to ensure that the Americans do not interfere in the lower continent. Suffice it to say we can't allow that to happen."

Powell hurried in with the chart.

"Light that lantern, if you please, Mister Powell," Donland said as he took the chart and laid it on the table.

Powell dutifully stuck a match. The additional lantern's light flooded the cabin.

"Here is Rio," Donland said and pointed.

Sumerford used his finger and traced through the harbor to a point well up the right side and stopped at a large cove. "Here!" Sumerford said. "They have six frigates under construction built on the plans of the American frigates. The lumber they are using is stronger and harder than oak. And they have plans to build four more. Two ships were nearing completion and ready to slip into the water when I left there. They await their masts, which were ashore and ready to be fitted. So you now understand my urgency of getting this information to Antigua. Whoever commands there must sail immediately to put a stop to those ships being built."

"Aye," Powell said. "Such a squadron as they are constructing would have the power and speed to decimate anyone who stood against them. Stopping them would require a fleet action."

"Aye," Donland said in agreement. "Sumerford, you have convinced me. If you had confided in me sooner, I would have already dispatched that worrisome frigate. But, that is in the past, tomorrow is another day."

Sumerford turned to Donland. "Now that you know and I'm sure those on the deck above us also know, it is all the more imperative that I arrive in Antigua. If you fail, and any one of your crew is captured and tells what they have heard, then we have no hope of stopping those ships from being built."

"Aye," Donland agreed and asked, "When did you depart Rio de Janeiro?"

"Nine weeks ago," Sumerford answered.

"That would be sufficient time to have set the masts on the completed frigate and enough time to have her rigging and sails in place. All that remained to be done would be the guns and the crew. I dare say she may be ready to sail."

"The guns are there, the *Viala* brought a shipment of cannon. I do not know how many, but surely not enough to arm all those new vessels," Sumerford said.

"French guns I would imagine, and more set to arrive at any time." Powell stated.

"Yes, that is a logical assumption Mister Powell, Sumerford said.

Donland considered the information and reached his own conclusions. He said, "By the time we reach Antigua one if not two of those frigates will be ready to put to sea. The others will be well on the way to completion. I estimate that it will take two months to gather a squadron capable of dealing with the threat and to set them off. Sailing time to Rio de Janeiro will be four weeks from Antigua, even longer if from Jamaica. So, the earliest those ships can be attacked is four months from now and by then two if not three will be ready to fight. Add to their guns those of the *Viala* you have a formidable force."

"Have we the ships?" Powell asked.

"We do," Donland answered. "However, I do not know if any have been recalled to England or sent elsewhere. But that is not our concern. Our task is to reach Antigua as swiftly as possible. We will sail at first light and make the best use of the winds available to us. If that frigate and her consorts stand against us, I will show no mercy and give no quarter."

"Aye!" Powell said enthusiastically.

Sumerford straightened, his face was hard in the lantern light. His words were sharp, "You've forced my hand and I'll not forget it and now that you know what I know there are consequences. No man on this vessel will be allowed off her or have any communication with anyone not aboard. When we reach Antigua you will hoist the yellow flag of fever. Is that understood?"

"Aye," Donland answered. He understood fully the reasoning behind the quarantine. Sumerford could not risk the French or the Portuguese being warned.

Furious winds, rain and seas pounded *Oxford* as she rose and fell on the mad sea. The gale was worse than any encountered en route to the Falklands. The winds were fighting one another, coming from aft for a few moments and suddenly changing to gust from amidships. Sails flapped overhead and more than a few of the sail-handlers lost nails and suffered broken fingers. The driving rain blinded all.

"How long will this persist?" Donland shouted through cracked lips and in a croaking voice.

"I don't know," Winslow shouted back as he held to the wheel trying to aid the two helmsmen. "I've not seen the like before!"

Donland had shed his boat cloak, as it was no more than a sodden weight around his body. His hat too had gone the way of the cloak. He doubted that Rowland would ever be able to put it to rights.

Another huge wave broke over the larboard bow. The cascade of water flung several men to the deck. Were it not for the lines tied around their waists, they would have been lost. Not even the hand-lines they had rigged were able to save three poor souls. The mizzen mainsail was in tatters and the hands were unable to subdue it, the blocks were jammed.

"This blasted wind is ripping us apart!" Powell shouted.

"Aye!" Donland answered as he clung to the rail. Another sharp gust of wind almost took him off his feet. *Oxford* was being thrown about like a toy boat in a millpond during a gale.

"Captain!" Andrews shouted as he approached. Donland did not fault him for not adding the usual pleasantries.

"How much water, Mister Andrews?" Donland shouted to the young lieutenant.

"Three feet and rising!" Andrews managed.

Oxford's bow plunged into a trough and a huge wave broke on her flooding the deck with cascading water. Seconds later her bow was heaved heavenward, it hung precariously and then plunged into another trough.

Andrews shouted, "All pumps are working!"

Donland shouted back, "Stay with them!" He drew a breath and shouted louder, "Stay with them!"

"Aye!" Andrews answered and departed for the relative security of the orlop deck.

A rouge wave lifted *Oxford's* bow, corkscrewed and dropped her into a trough. The larboard forward gun broke loose and careened across the deck crashing into the starboard railing and went over. The gun carried two men with it; they vanished in the wind-driven waves without anyone hearing a cry. Lieutenant

Brunson, hatless and ill tempered, began shouting orders to check the lashings on the other guns.

Oxford's bow rose and fell again and again. Donland was from the quarterdeck to the bowsprit as often as was Powell. They both shouted and cajoled the men, sometimes threatening, sometimes offering words of encouragement and at other times laying hands to the tasks. By nightfall the chaos lessened. His strength and the strength of the ship's company were spent.

The first bell of the first watch sounded. "The glass is turned," David called and attempted to make the log entry. His fingers were numb from the many hours in the cold rain. The lantern flickered so that it was difficult to make out what he had written.

The night was black and the sea boisterous. Donland stared ahead beyond the bow into the blackness. His body ached, his belly griped for want of food. He called, "Mister Welles, fetch the purser if you please!"

"Aye, Captain, David answered and set off below. He found Leeland in his cabin reading by lantern light.

"Beg Pardon, Mister Leeland, the Captain wants you on the quarterdeck," David said.

"Aye," Leeland answered. He asked, "Has the rain slackened?"

"It has, as has the wind, but it is still a nasty night. You'll need your cloak."

"Very well," Leeland answered and rose from the cot.

"Biscuits and rum!" Donland said when Leeland appeared on the quarterdeck. "A second tot once they've been fed!"

"Aye, Captain," Leeland answered and set off.

Donland said to David, "It is little enough but until these seas calm, it is the best I can do for them."

"Aye, Sir, and if they are half as hungry as I then the biscuits will be like kidney pie and beer."

Donland did not leave the deck. He took one of the hard biscuits and washed it down with a dipper of water. Rum was never to his liking.

Chapter Eight

Donland came on deck at four bells of the morning watch. He shaded his eyes for a moment as the sun peeped between the heavy clouds scudding across the sky. He clutched the railing as *Oxford* rolled violently to larboard. The sea was like a roiling cauldron.

A quick check of the sails showed that the mizzen had been repaired, and all sails were set. They were on a north by west heading.

Lieutenant Malcolm was supervising the repairs to the starboard railing. Others were busy repairing rigging and holystoning the drying deck. The pumps were manned, attempting to pump the nearly four feet of water out of the hull.

Powell looked as haggard as any man Donland had ever seen. "Mister Powell, did you not sleep?"

"Aye Sir, a bit," Powell answered with a twisted smile and rubbed his bristled chin.

Donland was about to send Powell below but the lookout hailed, "Ship on the starboard bow! No sails!"

"One of the Portuguese?" Powell asked.

Donland pulled a glass from the rack and put it to his eye. The heavy rolling sea made focusing difficult. He only managed a quick glimpse of a bare mast as she rose up on a wave. "Sloop," He said. "Perhaps one of theirs, we'll not know until we are closer."

"Are we to alter course?" Powell asked.

"Aye," Donland answered and turned to Winslow. "Three points to starboard, Mister Winslow, if you please."

"Aye, Captain!" Winslow answered.

"Beat to quarters?" Powell asked

The question brought a smile to Donland's lips. He answered, "No, Mister Powell, I dare say whoever is aboard that sloop will be pleased to see us. We'll not need to beat to quarters for they're already beaten. However, I would have Lieutenant Sharpe and his men on deck and the swivels manned. The marines will dissuade anyone aboard that sloop from mischief."

"Aye, Captain!" Powell answered and called "Mister Hornsby pass the word for Lieutenant Sharpe, if you please!"

"Aye, Captain!" Hornsby replied.

Donland kept watch on the sloop. She did not raise a sail or attempt to signal. Whoever was in command would surely know *Oxford* was drawing near to intercept.

"She appears to be a derelict," Hornsby stated.

Oxford slowed closed the distance to within a quarter-mile. Donland studied her but was unable to discern movement on the sloop's deck. He chose not to comment. Others, he knew, would be speculating. The rumor that she was a ghost ship would circulate below deck like wildfire.

Sharpe was standing nearby. He asked, "Captain, shall I station my men?"

Donland lowered the glass from his eye. "If you please, Mister Sharpe." He then called to Andrews who was in charge of the poop, "Prepare the swivels," Mister Andrews.

The lookout called down, "Men on the deck!"

Donland lifted the glass to his eye then lowered it. "Mister Winslow, alter course two points. We will pass her on the larboard beam."

"Aye, Captain!" Winslow answered and ordered the course correction. The helmsman replied and pulled on the big double-wheel.

Donland turned to Powell, "Mister Powell send two more up the mast and have one take a glass. I do not want to be surprised."

Powell's face showed surprise but he said, "Aye, Captain!"

Sumerford chose that moment to come onto the quarterdeck. He considered the bobbing sloop while lighting one of his cheroots.

"You have a thought, Mister Sumerford," Donland asked.

"Just one, is there a possibility of a trap?"

Donland smiled and answered, "Aye, there is that. She has no colors aloft and could be Portuguese, pirate or some other nationality. My supposition is that she is one of the Portuguese sloops. We are in no danger as long as I keep a good distance. The seas are high and dangerous, but I am sending Mister Powell across with sufficient force."

He turned back to Powell, "Prepare two boats if you please. If we meet no resistance, you are to board and ascertain her disposition," Donland said.

"Aye, Captain. Are the men to be armed?"

"That would be advisable, do you agree?"

"Better pistols and swords than fists," Powell answered with a touch of humor.

Donland turned back to Sumerford and smiled. "See the state of her masts and rigging? No captain would render his ship so helpless. She suffered the battering of wind and sea and I'm surprised she is still afloat. Notice if you will," Donland said and pointed, "How low in the water she is. I estimate that she is on the verge of going under."

Oxford reached the sloop's aft quarter and Donland called to Brunson who was standing in the waist, "We will spill our wind, Mister Brunson!"

"Aye, Captain!" Brunson answered.

Donland bellowed, "Brace the cross-jack yards square, haul up the foresail!"

He turned to Winslow, "Helm a-lee, if you please, Mister Winslow!"

"Aye!" Winslow acknowledged.

Donland watched as his orders were carried out and called, "Ease off all!"

"Back the mizzen!"

Oxford began to slow. Donland gauged the distance and called to Winslow, "Hold fifty yards off her beam!"

"Aye," Winslow replied.

"Mister Powell, swing out your boats!" Donland ordered.

"Beg pardon Captain, there's a man signaling," Hornsby said.

Donland turned toward the sloop. There was indeed a man waving a scrap of white cloth.

"Seems there will be no fight," Sumerford observed.

Donland did not reply, his attention was on the boats being swayed out. Once they were over the side he looked for the man waving, he was still there and seemed to be shouting.

"Boats away!" Midshipman Welles shouted from the waist.

The launch came into view, crested a wave and fell off into the trough. The oarsmen pulled hard, keeping the launch from broaching as the next wave rolled under. The second launch came into view following the first. The crews of both were struggling in the heavy seas. Donland feared one or both might be upended. He could do nothing but watch.

It took all of twenty minutes for the first boat to cross the fifty yards to the sloop. The man on the deck left his post and tossed a line down to Powell's boat. Three other men soon joined him on deck. As Donland watched the drama unfold he saw Powell emerge and climb over the gunnel. The men meeting him seemed to be welcoming a savior.

The men from the boat poured up and over the gunnel and fell in behind Powell. All were holding their weapons at the ready. Powell seemed to be conversing with the man who had shown the white cloth. Donland could hear nothing but did his best to read the men's body movements to understand what was occurring.

Four more men came up from below and made their way to Powell. Two others were helping one of the four. The man that was half-carried drew his sword and there was a flash of sunlight as the sword was presented to Powell.

"That does it," Sumerford said. "He's surrendered the vessel."

"Aye," Donland said without taking his eyes from the proceedings. He watched as Malcolm and a group of men broke from the group on deck and descended the hatch.

"Shall I stand the men down, Captain?" Lieutenant Sharpe asked.

"Aye, it appears Mister Powell has things well in hand," Donland answered.

Winslow asked, "We're drifting toward the sloop, do you want to maintain this distance or continue to drift closer?"

"Hailing distance, if you please Mister Winslow, no closer," Donland replied.

"Aye," Winslow said.

Oxford continued to lift and roll with the heavy sea, as did the sloop. The breaks in the clouds were becoming more numerous and the brief periods of sun warmed Donland's back.

Four bells rang out loud and clear. "The glass is turned," Shouted Simon.

"Make the log entry, Mister Vickers," Hornsby ordered.

Donland stood with his feet planted on the deck and his hands clutching the railing. Powell and the incapacitated man remained where they were but the others, Donland assumed, under Powell's orders were attempting some repairs.

"Mister Winslow, will this weather hold for the noon sighting?" Donland asked.

"According to the barometer it will, pressure is rising," Winslow answered.

Malcolm's head appeared in the hatchway and he came on deck and straight to Powell.

"We'll have some answers now," Donland said aloud.

After more than a minute of conversation, Powell turned to the railing and cupped his hands to his mouth. "Ahoy *Oxford*!" he shouted.

The two ships were about two chains a part yet Powell's bellow was barely heard.

"Ahoy, Mister Powell!" Donland shouted. "Report!"

Powell shouted, "Portuguese!"

Donland replied, "Aye!"

Powell shouted, "Captain dead!"

Donland shouted, "Send Malcolm!"

Powell responded, "Aye!"

"Beg Pardon Captain, shall I have the men fed?" Brunson asked.

"Yes, Mister Brunson, we will be lying-to until the sloop's fate is decided. I will go to my cabin and wait for Mister Malcolm to return. He is to report directly to me," Donland said.

"Aye, Captain," Brunson said.

Sumerford and Honest trailed after Donland.

Rowland was waiting inside the cabin door. He helped Donland out of his coat. "Rosita has prepared a hot meal for you, something quite different," he said.

Donland merely nodded and sat at the table.

Honest chuckled and said, "Aye, it is different and you've not tasted the like before."

"And I suppose you've already sampled?" Donland asked.

"Aye, I'd not have her feed you something I'd not eat."

"You'd eat a dead horse," Sumerford said as he sat.

Rosita entered carrying a serving tray and a pitcher. The motion of the ship was lively, so she placed the pitcher on the deck between her feet, handed Donland a tin cup from the tray and then picked up the pitcher and poured hot tea. Next she handed him a large hunk of bread covered in steaming pork with mustard sauce poured over it. "You will like very much," She said and smiled.

She then served Sumerford.

Donland took a bite and instantly he was warmed all over. When he swallowed the heat of hidden peppers asserted itself. He lifted the tin cup and drank.

Honest started laughing.

"Blast your eyes!" Donland managed between gulps of tea. He drank again and said, "You could have warned me." He finished the tea and ordered, "Fetch me a pitcher of water!"

"Aye, Captain, aye!" Honest said and rose from his chair.

Sumerford ventured a small bite. He chewed and said, "I've had similar in New Orleans. His face showed no sign of the food being overly spicy.

Donland studied the pork and bread and called, "Bring me more bread!"

"It will lessen the flavor," Sumerford warned and took another bite.

The bread was brought and Donland finished his meal. It was quite delicious, and he told Rosita so. "Next time you prepare this I would prefer fewer peppers. "Si, Captain," She said and smiled.

There was a knock at the door.

"Come!" Donland ordered and Malcolm entered with his hat in the crook of his arm.

"Mister Powell's compliments Captain, he sent me to report," Malcolm said.

"Is she Portuguese?" Donland asked.

"Aye, Sir, as are the other two sailing in company with her. All three vessels were to intercept us and prevent us from making contact with any other English vessels. The one officer who survived, he was second, said that his ship was separated in the night from the other two. He did not see them again," Malcolm reported.

"And what of her damage?" Donland asked.

Malcolm stated, "The lieutenant, sorry, Sir, I can't pronounce his name, said that they lost their foremast about midnight and the captain was washed overboard just after. It was only when quite a few others went overboard that the remainder of the crew lashed all hatches and stayed below, forty-two survived. As to the sloop, she lost eight of her guns; her hull appears to be intact, what we could see of it. There's better than four feet of water in her and they've but the one pump."

"What does Mister Powell recommend?" Donland asked.

"He asks for our wash pump. He said that if he can get the water out of her that she can be salvaged. Also, he asks that you send buckets and more men to form a bucket line."

Donland considered the request. Powell would want to save the vessel, it was in his nature. However, doing so would require time and slow their progress to Antigua. On the other hand, he could not abandon the distressed remainder of her crew nor did he desire to take them aboard *Oxford*. Claiming her for a prize was out of the question since they were not, as he knew, at war with Portugal.

Sumerford spoke up, "I suggest you send her to the bottom, crew and all! She sought to damage you and will only slow us."

"Aye," Honest agreed.

"Mister Malcolm you've best eat and see that the boat crew is fed. I'll not be sending you back across," Donland said.

"Aye, Captain," Malcolm answered and turned to go.

"You've made a decision?" Sumerford asked.

Donland replied, "I've not but I am inclined to do what can be done for the vessel before leaving her. It is almost time for the noon sighting and once I've fixed our location, I will decide."

"I make it forty-six, eight by fifty-nine, two," Winslow stated.

"Aye," Donland agreed and asked, "Mister Brunson?"

"Aye, forty-six, eight by fifty-nine, two."

Donland handed the sextant to Simon and said, "Enter it into the log, if you please."

"That gale took us well off our course but we've a good wind," Winslow stated.

"That it did, Mister Winslow. Let us plot where we are," Donland said and started for the chart room.

"Beg pardon, Captain, Mister Powell is signaling," Midshipman Aldridge said.

Donland halted and turned. Powell was standing at the railing of the sloop waving a speaking trumpet. He stepped to the quarterdeck gunnel and called, "Report!"

Powell put the trumpet to his mouth and shouted, "Water dropping! Need pump!"

Donland shouted, "Aye," and turned away.

Brunson asked, "Captain shall I send the wash pump?"

"No, Mister Brunson, not as yet," Donland replied and started off to rejoin Winslow.

"I fix us to be here, six hundred miles or so southeast of Montevideo," Winslow stated.

"That is near my estimate," Donland said and straightened from the table. "If this wind holds we should make up lost time and the miles we were blown off course."

"That is so but we will eventually have to take a more northerly course if you still intend to anchor in English Harbor."

"North by west for as long as the wind holds," Donland said.

"Aye," Winslow agreed.

There was a tap at the door and David entered. "Beg pardon, Mister Brunson's compliments, Sir. Mister Powell has asked about the wash pump."

"I'll come," Donland answered.

The first thing he noticed was that *Oxford* was no more than a cable distant from the sloop. The second thing was that the sea was calmer.

"Mister Brunson you may load the wash pump and as many buckets as we have into the boat, if you please. I will go across with the pump."

"Aye, Captain, I took the liberty to prepare it for transport. I'll have it swayed up and into the launch," Brunson said with a straight face.

"Aye," Donland replied as he turned his attention to the sloop. There were men in the rigging and it appeared they were about to attempt to fish the foremast. He knew it would take more than a day to do so and then another day to rig sails. Sumerford would not be in agreement to linger. He would be right in his judgement because the information about the French building frigates was pressing. Still, it would be better to have the sloop repaired and under his control than to face her and the frigate.

"A penny for your thoughts?" Sumerford asked.

"I was just thinking of the frigate and the other sloop," Donland replied.

Sumerford put his hands on the railing and gazed out beyond the bowsprit. He said, "Matters not as we know our responsibility. We've got to get my information to your overseers."

"Perhaps our fleet will arrive after the horse has left the barn," Donland mused.

Sumerford continued to gaze ahead and said, "Perhaps."

"Have you a map of the harbor and where the building is being done?" Donland asked.

Sumerford turned and merely replied, "Perhaps."

Brunson interrupted, "Beg pardon, Captain, the boat is ready."

"Aye," Donland said.

"Why did you ask about a map?" Sumerford asked before Donland took a step.

Donland faced and smiled, "It will useful for those who must plan the raid."

Sumerford smiled and said in navy fashion, "Aye, for those who plan the raid."

Powell and the Portuguese lieutenant were waiting as Donland climbed over the gunnel.

"Captain, I present to you Lieutenant Rajas, presently commanding His Majesty's sloop *Tego*," Powell said.

Donland returned the lieutenant's salute and extended his hand.

"He's speaks little English," Powell offered.

Donland nodded and asked, "How is she below?"

"A few inches less but with the addition of the wash pump I expect to keep her afloat. She'll make a nice prize."

Donland was quick and said, "No, Mister Powell, she'll not be a prize. We are not at war and I'll not claim her as salvage. We will endeavor to put her to rights and aid Lieutenant Rajas. He is after all not an enemy."

Powell's face showed surprise, and he was about to object but Donland asked, "Understood Mister Powell?"

Powell still held the words of protest on his tongue but answered, "Aye, Captain."

Donland turned his attention to the fishing of the mast. "Now, I see that you are attempting to fish the forward mast. Have you enough sail and rigging?"

"Not near enough but I believe enough to put a sail on it," Powell answered.

Donland nodded and said, "That will not do, Mister Powell, no it will not do for our friend. Whatever is needed you have my permission to secure it from *Oxford*."

Powell appeared stunned but replied, "Aye, Sir."

"Form up your bucket line and set men to that pump. I would that we are away from here by noon tomorrow," Donland said.

"Aye, Captain," He answered and asked, "and men?"

"As many as you need to put this vessel to rights," Donland replied.

"Aye, Captain, but I don't understand your reasoning," Powell said.

Donland smiled at Lieutenant Rajas and asked Powell, "Have you an interpreter?"

"Lieutenant Rajas speaks Spanish and has a man to translate to that language," Powell answered.

Donland faced Rajas and said, "Teniente Rajas, por favor sea mi invitado y cene conmigo esta noche. Tengo una excelente cocinera."

A stunned Rajas replied, "Si, Capitan, Si!"

"Enviaré un bote para ti," Donland said.

Rajas nodded and replied, "Si, Capitan."

Donland explained to Powell, "I've invited the lieutenant to dine with me tonight and he has accepted. You will of course dine with us. I will send Mister Andrews across to continue the repairs and pumping."

"Aye, Captain," Powell said.

Donland could not help but grin. He confessed, "Rosita has been teaching me Spanish."

"I was impressed." Powell said and asked, "Do you wish to go below?"

"I think not, you have matters well in hand. I will go back to *Oxford* and send more men. In the meantime learn all you can about the ship and the crew and come across while there is still light."

"Aye, Captain," he answered.

Sumerford was waiting on the quarterdeck as Donland came through the salleyport. "A pleasant visit?" he asked Donland.

"Better than expected. Let us go to my cabin for a glass."

"Something a foot?" Sumerford asked.

Donland smiled and led the way to the cabin. He did answer, "Perhaps," as the marine guard opened the door.

Rowland took Donland's hat and coat. "Rum, if you please, Rowland," Donland said.

"And you, Sir?" Rowland asked Sumerford.

"Wine," Sumerford answered then asked Donland, "What does *perhaps* mean?"

Donland took the mug of rum from Rowland and sipped. Rum wasn't his preferred drink but he desired something other than wine. He licked his lips and said, "I have asked the Portuguese lieutenant to dine tonight. While he is dining and I suspect sleeping aboard *Oxford*, you will have ample opportunity to do me a service."

"A service, that is surprising. Exactly what is this service?"

"Merely to do what you do best."

"And what is it that you assume to be one of my many talents?"

Donland took another swallow of rum. He grinned and said, "Snooping of course. While the lieutenant is away from his command, I would like for you to go through the logs and papers for any information concerning the Rio de Janeiro harbor and its defenses. Also, it would be helpful to have a copy of the Portuguese signals book and especially their recognition signals."

"You are assuming I can read their language."

"I know that you read both Spanish and French, I should think that their language would not be too difficult if you are given enough time."

Sumerford smiled and sipped his wine. He asked, "And why would such information be useful to you?"

Donland answered, "Not for me but for the commander of the squadron that will have to sail into the harbor and wreck those ships. Having those signals might allow a vessel to slip into the harbor while the squadron bombards the defenses."

"And that is how you would attack?" Sumerford asked.

"It would be one way. But, it depends on where those ships are being built. Are they close in the harbor?"

"Regrettable no, they are about four miles from the mouth of the harbor. The entrance is heavily defended and it will take a considerable fleet to force the entrance," Sumerford stated.

"So, the task would have to be done by stealth rather than brute force?"

Sumerford smiled, "That is true and I suppose the daring young captain Donland would desire to lead the raid?"

Rather than answer, Donland asked, "The map that you've drawn, does it contain details?"

"Enough," Sumerford answered. He sipped his wine and said, "And you desire to see it in order to plan your attack?"

"There will be no attack either led by me or anyone unless there is adequate information. That is why I want you to go aboard the sloop tonight. Will you do it?"

Sumerford drained his glass and set it on the sideboard. "As you said, one of my many talents, so yes I will forego the meal at your table and do as you desire."

Chapter Nine

Rajas and Powell were seated side by side and Lieutenant Sharpe and Doctor Trammel were seated opposite them. Donland chose the Doctor and Sharpe because they both spoke some Spanish. Sharpe understood right away why he was chosen to dine and asked, "Is there something you desire me to learn from the lieutenant?"

"Yes, all you can about Rio de Janeiro, in particular about guard boats and fortifications in and around the anchorage. Don't be obvious and wait until he's had several glasses of wine. I do not know if he has a wife but if he hasn't ask if he takes ladies on boat rides in the harbor or something similar so we gain information."

Sharpe nodded and asked, "Captain may I be so bold as to ask if you are planning a raid?"

"Merely weighting options, Lieutenant Sharpe," Donland answered.

The wine flowed freely, and each man ate more than his portion of the spicy food Rosita prepared for the occasion. Donland was aware that she enjoyed preparing her native dishes and sought to impress the Portuguese lieutenant. He felt she succeeded, and that was why the wine flowed freely, cooling the palates.

Lieutenant Rajas was half-carried and half dragged to the cot in Andrews' cabin at the conclusion of the evening. He was, as Donland expected, too fond of a drink and would therefore awaken in the strange confines of *Oxford's* hull.

Donland, as was his habit, was dressed and on the quarterdeck as the sun climbed over the horizon. The sea was calm, and the air was warming. Lieutenant Sharpe looking haggard and unshaven approached his captain.

"Well Mister Sharpe, how goes the war?" Donland asked.

"Sir, if you are referring to the one in my head, it goes badly."

"As I suspected Mister Sharpe. You did consume more than your share of wine but not quite the amount of our Portuguese friend," Donland stated.

"That is so, Sir but I did attempt to match him. I've not written that report you requested. Once my head is a bit clearer, I shall endeavor to do so."

"And I trust you will shave," Donland said.

"Aye, Captain once I can trust my hand to hold a razor."

Sharpe made to leave but Donland asked, "Did our friend take a lady on a moonlight boat ride?"

Sharpe grinned and answered, "Only back to his ship and did comment that the guard boat lieutenant was often in his cups as were those under his charge."

Donland smiled and said, "Well done and I trust your report will have other similar details."

"Aye, Captain, Aye," Sharpe answered and started for the hatch.

"We've a fair sou'east wind Captain," Winslow stated.

"But the question is, for how long Mister Winslow?" Donland asked.

"I can promise you till sunset but tomorrow there may be a change," Winslow said.

"Then we shall have to make do with what we have. I intend to continue nor' west for as long as we've the wind."

Winslow stepped close to Donland and asked softly, "Rio?"

"Aye," Donland answered just as softly as Winslow had asked.

"Good morning Captain Donland," Doctor Trammel said. "I see that last evening's dinner and frivolity had no ill effect on you."

"Good morning to you Doctor Trammel. I, like you, have a taste for good wine but not to the point of excess. I've found it best to keep a clear head when at sea for the enemy may be just over the horizon."

"That is admirable, Captain. Just as I must keep a steady hand for what might come from over the horizon. Speaking of the horizon, are we to continue north?"

"Aye, and as swift as possible," Donland stated.

Trammel squared his shoulders back, took in a deep breath and exhaled. He grasped the rail and said, "There was a good amount of conversation concerning Rio de Janeiro last night, I was wondering if we will call there?"

"Why do you ask?"

Trammel smiled, "I've not been there and would like to experience the city."

Donland replied, "Like you, I've not seen the city and in answer to your question, no we will not drop our hook there. I've decided to shepherd the sloop as far as possible without adding to our voyage."

"Beg pardon, Captain, Mister Andrews is signaling," Brunson said.

Oxford and the sloop had widened the distance between them during the night to just over three cables. Both vessels rolled gently on the swells and there was no hint of storm or gale. The blue-green sea stretched from horizon to horizon with only the shadows of the clouds to mar its surface. All in all, it appeared to be a perfect day for sailing.

"He reports he will be ready to get underway in two hours," Brunson stated.

"So soon," Donland said in surprise. "Andrews must have had the men at it all night. Signal, him to await orders."

"Aye, Sir," Brunson said and turned to Midshipman Vickers to bend on the signal.

"Boat putting over the side Captain!" Brunson announced.

"That will be Mister Sumerford returning," Donland said.

"Wind freshening, Captain" Winslow stated from his perch on the chest.

"Aye," Donland acknowledged.

"Mister Hornsby, go below if you please and rouse my guest. Invite him to my cabin," Donland ordered.

"Aye, Captain," Hornsby replied.

"Mister Brunson we will sail after Lieutenant Rajas has returned to his ship. Mister Powell will be remaining aboard her to assist the lieutenant."

Brunson did his best to hide his grin and managed, "Aye, Captain."

Lieutenant Rajas appeared as if he had dressed in a hurry. His face was heavily bristled and appeared haggard. The evening's activities seemed to have aged him five years.

Donland rose from his chair and extended his hand. "Lieutenant Rajas may I offer you something to drink?"

Rajas looked uncertain so Donland asked again in Spanish.

Rajas face wrinkled in disdain and replied, "Agua, por favor."

"Si," Donland said with a smile and called to Rowland, "A pitcher of water, if you please, Rowland."

While Rowland brought the water Donland said in Spanish, "Your ship is ready."

Rajas half-smiled as he took the glass of water from Rowland. "Si, gracias."

"We will accompany you to Rio de Janeiro. Lieutenant Powell will remain aboard to assist you," Donland stated in Spanish.

At that, Rajas appeared concerned. "No, no!" he exclaimed.

Donland half-smiled and said, "I insist because your vessel is in need of repair and may well sink if I remove my men. We will see you safely to port."

Rajas downed his water and said in English, "I find Capitan Morales, si!"

Donland carefully said in English, "His ship sank."

Horror crossed Rajas' face. "No!" He shouted.

"Si!" Donland said and added, "We go to Rio de Janeiro!"

Rajas resigned to his fate and replied, "Si."

Sumerford came in as Rajas was leaving. Both men ignored each other. Donland waited until Rajas was out the door before he spoke.

"The lieutenant is not happy that I have assigned Mister Powell to remain aboard his ship. I am not surprised for if I were in his position I too would be offended and feel like a prisoner. But, as the saying goes, keep your friends close and your enemies closer."

Sumerford half smiled and said, "Enemy is the correct word. I read written orders to the deceased captain. He was to assist in stopping me from reaching any English port. De Sèze signed the order. But that is not of consequence to you, you wanted the signals book which I obtained as well as their recognition signals."

"Truly you are a remarkable spy," Donland said with a broad grin.

"It was not difficult; you could have obtained the materials with your limited skills. Everything was kept in a locker in the main cabin. That fool of an officer should have dropped them overboard before your men came aboard."

Donland nodded and said, "Aye, that would have been my first duty. The Admiralty would have expected no less."

Sumerford sat in the chair and asked, "Have you brandy?"

"There on the sideboard," Donland said.

Sumerford rose from the chair, went to the sideboard and asked, "One for you?"

"No, I think not. We are to get underway in a few hours."

Sumerford poured his drink and sipped. He returned to his chair. "And your enemy?"

"He'll not cause a problem, there are more of my men aboard than his and Mister Powell collected all weapons and has them guarded. There is little Rajas can attempt."

Sumerford lifted his glass and downed the remaining contents. He asked after licking his lips, "What are your plans?"

Donland smiled and said, "The wind is fair for the coast of Brazil and the sloop will sail in company until we tack for Antigua. Providing we have no difficulties or are challenged."

"The signal books and the other documents I collected, you intend to turn them over to whatever admiral is in command?"

"I do, they will be needed should a raid be planned," Donland answered.

"You have no plans of your own?"

Donland knew exactly what Sumerford meant by the question. He answered with a question of his own, "Should I?"

Sumerford rose from the chair and returned to the sideboard. He asked as he refilled his glass, "Since you are sailing toward Rio, I could only guess that you intend to at least, as you say in the navy, look in. Am I correct that that is in your mind?"

Donland rose from his chair and said, "It is in my mind but I have no orders to that effect and I can not justify doing so at present. If events occur that give me cause to, as you say, look in, then I am not averse to doing so. But, I have no plans as yet."

Sumerford faced Donland. "I could insist and then justify it to their lordships."

"You could but it would be a gamble and one I'm not sure you are willing to risk. Let me suggest we not discuss this further until we are closing with the coast."

"Agreed, as long as you will make no plan without discussing it with me."

"Aye," Donland agreed.

* * * * *

The sloop followed in *Oxford's* wake. Rajas was seldom seen on deck and it appeared that Powell was continually on deck. Donland assumed the young Rajas had taken to wine rather than asserting himself as master of his ship. No doubt, Powell was enjoying having command of a sloop once again. He would not willingly let her go but when the time came he would do so.

Winslow and Donland completed the noon sighting and made their way to the chart room.

"Mister Winslow I make the distance to Rio de Janeiro to be another four hundred miles. What is your calculation?" Donland asked.

"Give or take a dozen miles," Winslow said.

"Five days more sailing?"

"Aye, if the wind holds but if not six. Tomorrow we should tack north or risk adding more days to reach Antigua."

Donland understood Winslow was fishing to know if they would continue to Rio de Janeiro. But, he was not ready to discuss what he intended. Sumerford, likewise pressed him for what he intended. He did not answer for he was not sure what he intended. The decision to press on to Antigua or to look in at

Rio tormented him. Sumerford was to dine with him in the evening and a decision had to be forthcoming.

Just after six bells in the afternoon watch the lookout shouted down, "Deck there! Sail fine on the starboard bow!"

Donland heard the hail while sitting at his desk writing a letter to Betty. It was only the third he had written in as many weeks. Hastily he closed the letter with the words *I love you most dear.*

"Your coat and hat Captain," Rowland asked.

"Aye, if you please," Donland said as he stood and put the letter in the chest that held *Oxford's* important papers.

"Two masts and no larger than a barque, appears to be a merchantman," Brunson said while handling Donland the glass.

"Possibly," Donland said as he took the glass. "We can expect such as we draw nearer the coast."

The distant ship did appear to be a small barque sailing north. He wasn't concerned about the ship but rather *Oxford's* nearest to the coast. Any passing vessel could report *Oxford* to authorities on the Brazilian coast or to a Portuguese naval vessel. It was time to alert Powell.

"Mister Brunson we will lie-to," Donland ordered.

Brunson's face revealed his surprise but he managed, "Aye, Captain!"

He then ordered David to hoist, *Captain repair aboard.*

David's face showed just as much surprise as Brunson's had.

"Aye, Captain," David answered and bent to the task of bending on the signal.

Sumerford who was lingering nearby came closer to Donland and asked, "Is something a foot?"

"Only my hand is being forced, and the time has come to make a decision."

"Mister Powell has acknowledged, Sir!" David announced.

"Mister Sumerford, let us retire to my cabin while I await Mister Powell," Donland said and led the way to his cabin.

Sumerford asked, "You signaled for the captain to come aboard, did you mean for Rajas to join us?"

"No and Mister Powell will know for certain that I meant for him to come and not Rajas. He is the one in command and if you have been observing the sloop, you would be aware of the absence of Rajas on the quarterdeck."

"I admit that I have not and found it curious that you did not seize the vessel when you first encountered it. She would be a feather in your cap and the prize money would have pleased your crew."

Rowland was waiting and helped Donland with his coat. Donland said once he was free of the coat, "We are not at war and the vessel could not be legally taken as a prize. However, there was nothing to prevent me from offering assistance and that is what I have done by placing Mister Powell aboard with sufficient men to sail her."

"Maintaining your options until the last?" Sumerford asked.

"Aye, until the last and I have now reached that point. You have asked me several times if I have a plan, I confess to having intent but no plan. As to options, I am prepared to place three before you when Mister Powell arrives."

"Then I eagerly await Mister Powell," Sumerford said and moved to the sideboard and began pouring brandy.

Chapter Ten

Sumerford, Winslow, Powell and Donland were seated at the table. Donland looked from one to another and said, "Deniability," he let the word hang. "If there is to be a raid by us or a force sent from Antigua, then there must be deniability. We are not at war with Portugal and I doubt justification could be made for the attack because the ships are meant for the French. My guess is that our lordships in London would make the decision as to attack or not. I believe by the time the information reaches them that the decision will be to allow the ships to be built and then use whatever forces are available to attack them."

"My thought exactly," Sumerford inserted.

Donland said, "Aye," and continued. "We have their signals book and know their recognition signals. These are invaluable if an attack is to be mounted within a few weeks but in six months those signals will probably be replaced. Mister Sumerford has seen the almost completed frigates and the ones under construction."

He turned to Sumerford and said, "If you please."

They each stood in order to study the rough drawn map on the table. It wasn't exact but it showed the Guanabara Bay, the city of Rio de Janeiro and the village of Niteroi. It was on the banks at Niteroi that the frigates were being constructed. The site was a large cove and well protected by headlands.

"They chose well," Powell said.

"That they did, a deep enough channel I image and I know for certain easy access to the forest," Sumerford added. "Look here," he said and put his finger in the cove. "That is where the completed frigate was waiting for her masts. If she is still there, then it would be difficult to sail in with a small force and sink her. I'm not sure it could be done with a fleet. The entrance to the bay has four forts and there are any number of naval vessels at anchor."

"What of the cove, are there defenses?" Donland asked.

"None, not that I saw at the time I was there," Sumerford answered.

"Mister Winslow let us see your chart," Donland said.

"Aye," Winslow answered and began to unfurl the chart containing Guanabara Bay. "I can't vouch for the soundings, but if there is a seventy-four in the bay then *Oxford* will have no difficulty."

"She'll not be going in there if we go," Donland said and began to study the east coast of the bay. "Appears to be a mix of high hills, swamps and tidal lakes," he said.

"Surely you do not plan a land raid?" Powell said.

"No, but what I am considering will require an escape plan. As I said in the beginning, deniability is of paramount importance. Any attack must be accomplished in a manner that leaves no trace of our intervention. We can not afford to start a war with Portugal. Therefore, no man can be left behind unless he is dead and we must be able to escape with our force intact.

Leaving by ship or by boat would be impossible once the fires are lit."

"You plan to use the sloop to get in and take a land route to escape," Powell said guessing the plan.

"Aye, once in the bay we sail to the cove and take to the boats. The sloop will be fired to destroy any ships that are completed. We'll then set fire to those still on the blocks and escape along the coast."

"A daring plan," Winslow said.

"Aye," Powell agreed.

"The question is will it succeed?" Donland asked.

They were silent for a minute before Sumerford answered, "I believe it to be a better plan than would come from London and have a greater chance of success for two reasons. First, there is the element of surprise and second, the force would be small. Once, into the bay, past the forts then you are almost to the cove, no more than two miles."

"You are of the opinion that we should proceed?" Donland asked.

"I am and will state in my reports that I ordered you to do so under the authority that was given to me," Sumerford said.

Donland looked into the faces of each man then said, "The first task will be the transfer of Rajas' men to *Oxford*. After that preparations must be made for the attack, men assigned, weapons prepared, power and fuses stored, boats hoisted aboard the sloop and a plan of escape."

"Who will command?" Powell asked.

"Your captain will," Sumerford stated.

"Aye," Donland agreed. "Mister Powell, I will entrust *Oxford* into your capable hands."

Powell showed no surprise. He merely replied, "It is a risky venture, Isaac."

"It is and if we are not successful, then you may well benefit," Donland answered and smiled.

Powell spent the morning aboard the sloop supervising the exchange of crews. He had determined that Rajas would go in the first boat. The man was drunk and had to be roused from his bunk in the main cabin. He protested loudly about having his ship stolen but was subdued and loaded into the launch. The remainder of the crew went down into the boats without complaint.

Oxford's two launches were secured on the sloop's deck and room was made for the jolly boat. Powder, weapons and the makings for torches were sent over and stored.

Donland chose the men for the raid. He was very particular to choose men that were not slackers and idlers nor men overly fond of rum. Bill Freedman and his mates were his first choices, he trusted them and they him. As to the others, he chose the young and most fit. He knew that the trek from Niteroi would be hazardous. The distance would be just over ten miles but the terrain would be jungles and swamps. It was not a journey for the old or the crippled and for that reason he chose Hornsby, Andrews and Malcolm. David pleaded to be allowed to join the raid but he was ordered to remain.

The bell clanged six times in the forenoon watch. Donland watched as Powell climbed down into the boat and gave the order to "give way all".

He was not surprised that Sumerford came up from the hatch dressed in seaman's garb and carrying a small sack.

"I see that you intend to join the expedition," Donland said.

"That I do and I must confess that I am dressed somewhat more shabbily than you."

"Aye, it is not quite a comfortable fit but for the purpose it will be sufficient."

"Quite true, as long as you are not discovered for being an imposter. The Portuguese will not take kindly to you wearing one of their uniforms." Sumerford said and fished in his pocket for a cheroot and a match.

"I believe the penalty is to be shot as a spy," Donland said with a straight face.

"That it is old son so I will do my utmost best to keep you from discovery."

"Your kindness will be appreciated and I will endeavor to be as considerate for your health and welfare."

"Beg pardon, Captain, the boat is ready," Powell stated.

"Aye," Donland answered and started for the salleyport.

The Portuguese naval uniform fit Andrews remarkably well. He saluted as Donland climbed onto the deck. "All is in order Captain and prepared to sail."

"Aye, Mister Andrews. Let us be about it."

"Aye, Captain!" Andrews answered.

"Loose the heads'ls!"

"Hands aloft to loose the tops'ls!"

He waited and watched then ordered, "Sheet home!"
"Hands to the braces!"

The sails began to fill and billow. The sloop tilted slightly to the press of wind.

The hard slapping of hurrying feet on the deck was music to Donland's ears. The shouting and cursing of those climbing the shrouds and the rigging were reminders of a time past.

"Steerage!" the helmsman shouted.

"Helm steer nor'west!" Donland ordered.

The little sloop brought back memories of *Hornet*. He could almost see burly Jackson stomping up and down the deck shouting, ordering and kicking arses. And then there was the mountain of a man Samson, long gone now, as tender a man that ever lived. Donland put away the memories; stood enjoying the freedom of the little sloop set free and the rush of wind and the bursting of her bows through waves.

"Beg pardon, Captain, signal from *Oxford*, enemy in sight," Hornsby said.

"Aye, Mister Hornsby, no need to reply for we are that enemy," Donland said with a wry smile. "Two men on the mainmast, if you please. We do not want to be caught unaware."

"Aye, Captain," Hornsby answered.

He turned to Andrews and asked, "How is it below?"

"Less than a foot in her now and my nightfall we should know if there are leaks."

"Keep the men at the pumps until she is as dry as possible. If a leak is discovered we'll not bother with it. My only concern is getting her into that bay, after that, hopefully we will be ashore."

Sumerford interrupted, "I am going below, is there a fit cabin?"

"Honest, go below with Mister Sumerford, find him a cabin," Donland ordered.

"Aye Captain," Honest answered and followed after Sumerford.

"Now, Mister Andrews, the guns?"

"We've six six-pounders, twenty-two balls and plenty of power. Shall I exercise the men?"

"No, I think not, keep all hands on deck until nightfall. We've not men enough to handle sail and guns and that jury-rigged foremast might carry away. I want to make use of every scrap of canvas we have for all long as we have it. If we are forced to use the guns, I have no doubt you will manage."

"Aye, Captain," Andrews answered.

"Two men in the chains to cast the log, if you please. We must set the pace for *Oxford*. If it is to appear to be a chase, we can't be seen to be outpacing her." Donland said.

Donland remained on deck for the better part of the hour. The sloop was every bit the racehorse that *Hornet* had been. Even with the damaged foremast she was managing four knots. Given time she would easily out distance *Oxford*. Sails and rigging were adjusted so that, to the eye, the sloop was managing her maximum speed when in fact she wasn't. But it had to appear she was just barely keeping her distance from *Oxford*. Everything might well depend on it.

"There's no wine aboard only this pissy watered rum," Sumerford said as Donland removed his coat.

"Fitting for this voyage, nothing is as it appears to be," Honest said.

"For once, I will agree with you," Sumerford answered.

"Is the cabin suitable?" Donland asked.

"A pig's sty, but I've slept in worse. This one appears to be no better, just larger.

"I'm sure than when the captain of this vessel lodged here that it was more to your liking. However, Lieutenant Rajas showed no inclination toward cleanliness or order. I expect he owed his position to favor not merit," Donland said.

"He'll not like the hold aboard *Oxford*," Honest mused.

"He may not," Donland said and added, "but he is alive and that counts for something."

Donland sat at the table and looked across to Sumerford, "Mathias, what are your plans after this business is concluded?"

Sumerford pushed away the tankard. "You mean if I survive this business. If so, I've had my quota of cold miserable weather, treachery and service for king and country. I will retire to the life of a gentleman among the gentle people of Charleston, perhaps even marry."

Honest burst into laughter.

The statement brought a smile to Donland's lips. "I agree with you about the cold. My bones do not take kindly to it and I'd care not be so far south again. As to marriage, I scarcely can imagine you married. Is there a lady that I've not met?"

Sumerford finished fishing out his cigar case and struck a match. As he blew blue smoke he said, "You've met her. Ellen Calhoun, a widow with two children."

"You are to be bride and father all at once. Any chance either or the children are yours?" Honest asked.

"Honest, sometimes you go too far, too far by half!" Sumerford said and glared at Honest.

"Aye," Honest replied in the way of an apology.

"Yes, I do believe I met the lady, slightly tall with green eyes and auburn hair?" Donland asked.

"That is her sister. Ellen was the shorter of the two with blue eyes and her hair a shade lighter," Sumerford answered.

"Have you asked her to marry you?"

"I have and she has agreed. The wedding will be announced upon my return. We will take up residence just outside the city in her country home. She doesn't enjoy the house in the city and only maintains it for social gatherings."

"Beauty and wealth," Donland mused.

"Not so much wealth, in fact she was facing eviction until I secured the property. Her husband was a gambler, losing the family fortune and incurring substantial debt. I loaned her what was needed, but mind you, this was after I asked for her hand."

"Then you've reason to take no chances on this venture," Donland said.

"That is true, I've reason but like you, I've duty and the risks must be borne. I can say that when I left Charleston that I did not leave with expectations of facing cannons. I embarked with the expectation of returning in a few months with a useless report to be filed and forgotten. Rumors being what they are in this age, even the reported impeccable source of the information did not completely sway me."

"I agree I'd not have put much stock in the Portuguese building frigates for the French."

Sumerford blew smoke and asked, "What of you? Will you marry my cousin?"

Donland considered the question. He answered after a moment saying, "We've discussed it before *Hornet* was sold.

We've not discussed since I've received *Oxford*. And now, with war with France a possibility, my future is even more uncertain."

"You've made no commitment," Sumerford stated.

"I've not." Donland admitted.

"I see your dilemma in that she is an American and you are a serving British officer and may well be called to England to stand against the French. She will not want to leave her life and family to live in England on her own."

"That is the way of things," Donland said and sighed. "If it were possible I would purchase a home in Charleston, marry her and be content but it is not as easily done as saying it."

Sumerford laughed and said, "Oh but it is Isaac, you just have to do it. The Crown will not suddenly dissolve without you defending it from your quarterdeck. In fact, the King would not miss you no more than a dog would miss a single flea. And, once free of this yoke, you have opportunities you have not considered."

"He'd not give up command no mor'n you'd give up breathing!" Honest inserted.

"Honest, that I'd not care to do," Sumerford said. "But I do understand. A life's dream fulfilled is no easy thing to throw upon the trash heap. It is as I've always heard; a sea captain is married to his ship and takes a mistress on the land."

"Aye," Donland agreed. "The love of one is always in conflict with the other."

A knock sounded at the door and Hornsby came in. "Beg pardon, Captain, signal from *Oxford*. There's a sail on the horizon to her north."

"I'll come up," Donland answered and stood. He reached for his coat.

"Another signal, Captain," Andrews said as Donland cleared the hatch.

"Read it Mister Andrews," Donland ordered.

Andrews lifted his glass and said, "Ship has altered course and is closing."

"Acknowledge, Mister Andrews!"

"Aye, Captain!"

Donland considered the situation. The sighting may well be the Portuguese frigate or the other sloop. There were other possibilities but none as likely.

"Mister Hornsby send up, *Make more sail, maintain course!*"

"Aye, Captain, in our flags or theirs?"

"Ours Mister Hornsby, Lieutenant Powell would not know theirs!"

"Two hours until nightfall, Captain," Andrews observed.

"Aye, I've taken that into consideration. That vessel will not be in firing range until then and before that, Mister Powell will make her out."

"You suspect her to be that frigate?"

"Either her or the other sloop, Mister Andrews. The question will be what to do with her when the sun rises. We will be within a half-day sailing time of the coast. I'd not want to fight her so near our destination but it appears we may have little choice."

The next signal from *Oxford* identified the vessel as a two-masted sloop.

Just before the sun disappeared *Oxford* signaled, *sloop lying-to! Frigate closing!*

"We have our answer, Mister Andrews," Donland said and was pleased. "The captain of the frigate has ordered the sloop's captain to lie-to and wait. I'm sure that will gall that captain to have to wait until morning."

"How is that good for us?" Andrews asked.

Donland smiled and said, "By the time the frigate reaches the sloop we will have increased the distance between us by several miles. If we continue to sail through the night, it is unlikely that they can recoup the distance. *Oxford's* task in all of this is to chase us into the bay making the Portuguese think their sloop is being chased. They will not be concerned with the likes of us once they see that we only have one mast and appear as we've sustained damage. At the first shot from the shore battery,

Oxford is to haul off and await our party up the coast. The frigate and the sloop will probably give chase but I've little doubt that Mister Powell will deal with them."

"We've a half moon tonight and no cloud," Andrews said.

"I've considered that as well. If I am correct, our plan will remain unchanged."

Andrews gazed out at sea then turned back to Donland and asked, "What of our preparations?"

Donland pursed his lips and said, "Nothing has changed. As we close with the roads, we will hack down the fished mast and allow it to go over. Anyone observing will think that it was hit by one of *Oxford's* balls. They will be none the wiser as to our intent."

"So we sail safely in under their guns."

"That is so Mister Andrews."

Andrews smiled and said, "We are the Trojan horse."

"Exactly, Mister Andrews."

Chapter Eleven

Oxford maintained her distance through the night giving the appearance of giving chase. Donland was pleased that his plan was still intact. The frigate and the sloop were seven miles distant from *Oxford* and closing. Several smaller sails were sighted close in shore and were most likely traders and fishermen.

The next four hours were crucial. Donland instructed those making up the torches not to dawdle. He also ordered that the casks of power and the fuses be laid. In two hours time, they would reach the roads leading into the bay. *Oxford* by then would be in range of the frigate's guns. Whether or not the captain would fire on *Oxford* was still unanswered. He would have justification the moment *Oxford* fired on the presumed Portuguese sloop.

Heavy clouds were rolling out to sea from the land. The wind, however, remained favorable to run into the bay. It would be only a matter of time before the weather pushing out to sea robbed the sloop of wind. *Oxford* would have to contend with changing winds once she made her northern tack.

Sumerford came on deck bearing a tankard and a hunk of bread. "I thought you might need something before the activities of the day become strenuous."

"Aye, thoughtful of you," Donland said as he took the tankard. "Rum?" he asked.

"And flavoring from my flask," Sumerford answered.

"Not so much that I lose my head, I trust?"

"A weaker man perhaps would but I rather think that with all that you contend with that it will only fortify you."

Donland bit off a chunk of bread and began to chew. It had a familiar taste. "From Rosita?" he asked.

Honest answered before Sumerford could, "Aye, she sent the bread."

The lookout called down, "Big ship!" and pointed with his outstretched arm.

Donland took another bite, chewed and swallowed then lifted the tankard and gulped the mixture. "Mister Hornsby, what do you see?" he called to Hornsby who was high on the shrouds with a glass to his eye.

"It's the seventy-four; she's anchored about a half-mile into the bay."

Ahead the bay was opening up. On the headland nearest their approach was a fortress. Flags soared up a mast.

"Come down Mister Hornsby and send the two lookouts down as well," Donland ordered.

He then turned and studied *Oxford*, he was just over a mile distant. Past her he could make out the frigate about another two miles distant.

"Ready with the axes!" Donland called to those at the foremast.

No sooner had he spoken than there was cloud of smoke wreathing *Oxford's* bow.

"Now!" Donland shouted.

The two men with axes hacked at the ropes holding the fished mast in place. It took several seconds but then in slow motion it began to tilt and then the crack of parting lines sounded like a half-dozen pistols shots.

"Cut those lines before it drags us around!" Donland shouted

Men jumped into action and began hacking at the lines still binding the mast to the ship. It fell away cleanly.

"Mister Powell must have added whale's oil to that shot to produce so much smoke," Andrews remarked.

"Aye!" Donland replied. He had not thought of doing so. It was a good touch to the drama.

"Guns!" Hornsby shouted. "The fort is firing on *Oxford*!"

Curious as to the reaction of the frigate, he turned to see that she was closing fast but did not appear to be firing. It would come, he told himself. "Now, Powell!" he said under his breath. He watched paying no heed to the fortress until *Oxford's* sails began to go round. Seconds later Powell ordered the starboard battery to fire on the frigate. There was no visible damage.

"We've lost a knot," Donland heard Hornsby said.

They had reached the headland and the entrance to the bay was open before them. The guard boat sat directly ahead in the middle of the bay.

"Fortress asks the recognition signal," Hornsby called.

"Send it up, Mister Hornsby and say a prayer as you do!" Donland ordered.

"Aye," Hornsby answered and bent to the task.

Donland checked on *Oxford*. She was well into her tack northward. Without warning she fired and was instantly wreathed in smoke. Powell fired the lower battery of big guns. The heavy balls found their marks and shredded the frigate.

"Huzza! Huzza!" the cry went up from those on the sloop's deck.

"Belay that! Tend your tasks!" Donland shouted.

"Fortress acknowledged!" Hornsby shouted.

"We're through then!" Sumerford said to Donland's back.

"Two points north," Donland ordered the helmsman.

He shouted to the men on deck, "Ready the boats!"

Turning, he took one last look at *Oxford*, perhaps his last, she had completed her tack. The frigate had lost her mizzen and her sails were being brailed up. Her fight was over. The other sloop appeared to be luffing.

Donland realized he still held the tankard and lifted it to his lips. "So far so good, dear Lord," he thought.

"Masts Sir, looks to be two ships. One is rigged with sails," Andrews shouted.

Donland looked and called to the helmsman, "Steer well larboard of the headland!"

"Mister Andrews, two men in the chains, if you please, we must not go aground now!"

"Aye, Captain," Andrews answered.

Honest announced, "*Oxford* has cleared the headland, seems without damage!"

"Brail up the main!" Donland ordered.

The remaining men on deck bent to the task. Those in the waist were busy preparing the boats for hoisting over. Sumerford stood nearby one of the boats looking like a pirate with two pistols in his belt, powder horn and sword. He wore a blue bandana around his head.

"Haul!" Andrews shouted to the men clewing up the main'sl.

Donland stood by the helmsman waiting to order the boats over.

"By the mark six!" a man in the chains shouted.

The second man on the opposite side of the sloop cried out, "Deep six!"

The main'sl was secured and their speed was reduced by half. Overhead the sky was darkening with heavy cloud.

"We've not much time," Honest observed.

"Aye," Donland agreed. "We best be at it."

"Boats away, Mister Sumerford!" Donland shouted.

Sumerford said to the men nearest him, "You heard the Captain, put them over!"

The first boat was hoisted up and swung out with two men sitting in it. As soon as it hit the water the boat was unhooked and men began climbing down into it. They carried with them torches, small kegs of power, fuses, pistols and their knives. Once across to the land they would have to follow a trail just over a half-mile to the ways where the ships were under construction.

The second boat was hoisted out and over. Donland watched as Sumerford climbed over the gunnel and down into the boat. He wondered if the wedding would really take place. Andrews was the last to climb down.

"Mister Hornsby, hoist out the jolly boat and tie her off!" Donland ordered.

"Aye Captain!" Hornsby answered,

"By the mark five!" the linesman called. His mate called, "Half-past five!"

They were gliding along under the top's'l's maintaining steerage and not much more.

The rumble of distant thunder caught Donland's ear. He was watching the first boat make landfall. The second was coming up close behind. He had only eight men remaining aboard the sloop. In minutes they would be near the point of tacking.

"Deep four!" the linesman called.

"So far, so good," Donland whispered as lightening flashed. "Prepare to tack!" He shouted.

"Linesmen on deck help with the tack!" he ordered.

"Honest prepare to light the fuses!"

"Aye, Captain!" Honest said and hurried down into the waist.

The fuses were laid to several kegs of power in the waist and on the foredeck. One fuse also ran down to the magazine.

"Tack!" Donland ordered.

"Helmsman, hard over to starboard!"

"Aye, Captain!" the man answered.

"Haul!" Donland shouted to the men manning the lines.

The men began to haul on the lines to bring the top'sl yard around. Donland watched and waited. Slowly the bow began to turn. He willed it to turn faster. The wind from the storm blowing in from inland was gusting. One gust suddenly billowed the sails and the sloop's deck tilted.

"Belay hauling!" Donland shouted

The sloop still continued her turn being forced by rudder and sail. She was coming round.

"Put the boat over!" Donland shouted!

"Helm! Hard over to larboard!"

"Aye, Captain," the man answered and pulled hard on the wheel. He struggled so Donland laid his strength to the task.

The bow now was aimed straight for the two frigates that were anchored side by side.

"Hold her here, sail between them!"

It was perfect, just room for the sloop to glide in and ensnare herself in the rigging of the completed ship.

Donland gauged the distance and speed, "Tie off the helm!" he ordered.

"Aye, Captain," the helmsman answered.

Donland called to those putting the boat over, "Down into the boat!"

The sloop was no more than fifty yards from the aft quarter of the frigate. Just time enough for the men to get clear after lighting the fuses. He could hear the crackle and bang of muskets and pistols from somewhere on his left. Andrews, Sumerford and Malcolm were probably fighting for their lives as they put torches to the ways and the other works. He only hoped enough would survive to place the casks of power and light the fuses. As he glanced, up he saw dark storm clouds racing by. He smiled for he knew the winds would fan the flames of the fires being set.

He called down to the waist, "Honest light the fuses!"

"Aye Captain," Honest answered and lit the cheroot that Sumerford had given him.

Lightening again flashed and was followed seconds later by a tremendous boom. It didn't sound like thunder. The boom was followed by a second and then an even larger rumbling that he decided was really thunder. The first two booms were casks of power going off on the ways.

Honest lit the first fuse using the cheroot and picked up the second. Finally, he lit the third. All three were burning and hissing.

The yards of the frigate were now looming overhead and without warning there was the sudden grinding crunch as the hulls ground against one another. Overhead came the sound splintering wood. The hulls continued to grind together and Donland looked up to see men on the frigate's deck. They began aiming muskets and fired. Two balls splat the planking near his feet. The sounds of the shots were indistinguishable to the lines in the rigging parting. A block falling from the mainmast almost hit Honest as he raced up the ladder to the quarterdeck.

A ball plucked at Donland's trousers. "We must get over the side," he shouted to Honest.

"Aye," Honest shouted as he swung up onto the gunnel and leaped.

Donland was right behind him. The first powder keg blew sending gun wadding and slivers of burning wood high into the rigging of all three ships. Donland splashed down into the warm waters and went under. He began fighting his way to the surface and realized that his boots and the baggy trousers were hindering him. Putting the toe of one boot against the heel of the other he managed to dislodge the boot. The second boot was not as easily managed and he was almost out of breath but the boot slid off and he fought his way to the surface.

Honest was waiting. "Thought old Davy Jones had you by the short ones!"

"Aye, the blasted boots filled with water," Donland managed while treading water. It was at that moment that the sloop's magazine exploded. The shock wave slammed Donland and Honest against the frigate's rudder. Both went under and as they came up, found themselves in a rain of timber, shards, and burning embers. Were it not for the overhang of the frigate's hull both would have perished. They clung to the rudder until the rain ended.

"Where's the bloody boat?" Honest shouted.

Donland did a half-turn and finally saw it, some twenty yards away. "There!" he shouted. The jolly boat or what was left of it was burning. He saw heads bobbing in the water, either dead or alive. He couldn't tell.

"We have to swim for it!" He shouted to Honest.

"Aye," Honest replied and turned loose of the rudder.

Donland gazed up at the sloop. She was engulfed in flames, as was the frigate. Men on the frigate were jumping overboard. He began to swim for the shore and reckoned it to be fifty yards away.

"Honest can you swim that far?" He asked as he stopped to tread water.

"I've a plank!" Honest shouted back over his shoulder.

Donland turned in the water and found a large piece of timber. "Aye," he called. "I've one now!"

Something snagged Donland's trouser leg; he turned and saw a head. Reaching out he grasped the hand and pulled, it was Abbot, the helmsman. The man half-smiled and said, "Thank ye, Sir, thank ye."

"Here, take hold!" Donland said to Abbot. He asked, "Are you injured?"

"Busted rib maybe," Abbot said through clenched teeth.

"Can you kick?"

"Aye, I think so!"

They reached the shore just behind Honest and three others. Each man lay on the small beach gasping for air. Four other men emerged from the bay and flopped down on the beach. More than a minute passed before Donland ordered, "On your feet lads, we've got to find our mates!"

He rose on one knee; a huge explosion shook the air. Turning he witnessed the sky over the completed frigate filled with flames, timbers, and other debris. "They put powder aboard her!" He was then hit with a rush of hot wind and sand. Managing to get onto one knee again he saw that the sloop was gone, and the frigate was sinking fast. The other frigate was burning like an old thatched house ablaze. Neither ship would be salvageable.

"Yonder, Sir!" Honest shouted.

Donland faced where Honest pointed and saw flames shooting above the trees. There were three small explosions in quick succession and heavy black smoke drifted over the trees. The rain came then, heavy drops beating down.

"On your feet, we best be away!" Donland ordered. He started off at a trot.

"Move your arse," Honest shouted to one of the men.

"You men have knives?" Donland asked over his shoulder as he ducked under a bush.

"Aye, I've mine," Honest answered and three others also called they had their knives.

"Be ready!" Donland shouted and began making his way between trees and bushes. He knew that to reach the mainland that they were to have the flames and smoke at their backs and that they would intercept a road some hundred yards along the edge of the cove.

The rain became a deluge drowning out all other sounds as it hammered down on the trees and the large fronded bushes. Donland thought how it resembled an eerie silence. He halted the men at the edge of the road. "This way!" he shouted and led off at a fast walk. The rain slackened to no more than a sprinkling. The only information he had as to where they were going was from a rough map that Sumerford had drawn. Somewhere ahead was a cantina on the left. That was to be their rendezvous. From there, they were to find a track that led inland, over several hills and down to the coast. It wasn't much information but it was all they had.

The abrupt crack of a pistol shot pierced the rain. Donland instantly cowered and leapt to the edge of the road. Behind him, the men were slower to do as he had. They rattled the brush as they sought cover. He peeked from behind a bush but could not see anything. The pistol that was lodged in his belt before he jumped from the sloop was gone; he only had the dirk. "Follow me, stay close to the edge," he turned and said to Honest.

"Aye," Honest answered and began to follow.

A heavy burst of rain came and then slackened. Ahead, he was able to see a group on buildings straddling the road. He reasoned that one of them would be the cantina. As he drew near, he saw movement. Cautiously, he stepped back into the bushes and watched. Two men with tall hats and muskets pushed a third man out into the street.

"Honest, come with me, you others wait for my signal," Donland whispered.

"Aye," Honest replied and stepped out behind Donland. The pair then walked side by side out into the middle of the road and Donland leaned on Honest's shoulder. Donland whispered, "Hold me up like I'm injured, they'll recognize the uniform coat and won't challenge us."

"Aye," Honest answered.

One of the two men smashed the butt of his musket into the prisoner's back and sent him sprawling onto the wet sand. Neither noticed Donland and Honest until they were within ten feet or so. The shorter of the two swung round with his musket and said something. He then suddenly shouted at his companion and came to attention.

With the suddenness of a coiled snake, Donland brought the dirk from behind his back and rammed it into the short Portuguese soldier's stomach. Honest flung his knife, and the blade plunged into the other man's chest. Donland then punched and kicked his man to the ground and withdrew the dirk. In the next instant he picked up the man's musket. Honest bent and gripped the other musket.

The man on the ground groaned and began to sit up. Donland was shocked to see Malcolm staring up at him. "Are you injured?" he asked.

"Aye, Captain, the bugger sliced the back of my leg."

Donland bent down and tore away the trouser leg. As he was binding the wound he asked, "Where are the others?"

"I was limping along when they caught up to me. There are a dozen or so giving chase. Mister Andrews and the others are ahead of them."

"Then let us give chase," Donland said as he helped Malcolm to his feet and said. "Honest, you take him." He then plucked the dead man's pouch of powder and shot.

Malcolm appeared to be in a great deal of pain but gamely tried to carry his own weight. Donland doubted he would survive the wound unless he soon received a surgeon's attention. The slice was almost to the bone. Still, he could not leave the young officer to die alone.

The rain ended as they made their way along the narrow track that soon turned into mud and became slippery as they ascended a steep hill. Honest and Malcolm fell twenty feet behind Donland and the others.

"Halt!" Donland commanded.

"Captain, you go on ahead, we'll catch up!" Honest said.

"We go together or not all," Donland answered. He draped Malcolm's arm over his shoulder and he and Honest more or less carried the young man. Once they reached the top, either a pistol or a musket shot sounded at the bottom of the hill.

"They'll be needing these muskets," Donland stated.

"Aye," Honest said and added, "Leave me a man, Mister Malcolm and I will manage."

Donland didn't argue. "Take the musket," Donland ordered the man next to him and began to trot down the hill. Rounding a sharp bend in the trail he almost stumbled over a wounded soldier. The man was clutching his belly. Donland stared down at the man and the musket lying beside him.

"Take his musket and pouch!" Donland told another of the men.

"Poor bugger!" the man said as he picked up the musket.

The man said nothing nor moved to stop him.

Another shot echoed from ahead.

"Follow me," Donland ordered as he started off at a fast walk. Rounding a large tree the acrid smell of a freshly fired weapon stung his nose. He slowed and whispered to those behind him. "Check the power!" He prayed it was dry enough to fire.

The bang of a musket echoed. They were close. Movement caught his eye, a tall hat. He saw two more hats peeking from cover. A shot rang out; it was further down the track. Evidently one of Sumerford's party had seen a target.

"See him?" Donland asked the man behind him.

"Aye," the man answered and aimed the musket. He fired, his target's back arched as the ball tore into him. The second man turned, bringing up his musket to return fire.

There was a blast from behind Donland as one of his men fired, the ball caught the second man in the shoulder and spun him around. There arose shouting and movement as the Portuguese soldiers sought cover from the threat at their rear.

Donland dove behind a tree just as a volley of three shots plucked at foliage around him. It was exactly what he wanted, he shouted as loud as he could, "*Oxford* to me!"

"At em' lads!" Donland heard Andrews shout.

A pistol cracked and Donland knew it was probably Sumerford firing one of his two pistols.

He rose from his tree and pulled his dirk and ran headlong toward the fighting. The men followed shouted and bellowed as they ran. One soldier attempted to escape by running back toward the cantina; Donland ducked a wild swing of the man's musket and sliced him across the ribcage. He went down screaming.

"Captain!" Andrews said as the two came face to face.

"Aye," Donland answered.

Sumerford slipped past Andrews, he was grinning and said, "I thought it was you when I heard that musket shot."

"And I knew it was you when I heard that pistol shot," Donland said and grinned."

"Captain, Mister Malcolm needs his wound bound," Honest said as he more or less dragged Malcolm.

"Aye," Donland said as Honest laid Malcolm on the ground.

Sumerford said, "Let me, I've a bit of experience."

Donland stood as Sumerford began to staunch Malcolm's bleeding. "How many men have you?" he asked.

"All but four, we torched everything and were making our way toward the road when the soldiers appeared. These are what were left but I would assume there will be many more after us."

"Aye," Donland said. "We are leaving a trail of dead."

"Did you burn the frigates?" Andrews asked.

"One blew up and I'm certain the other burned and sank, their lordships will be pleased."

Sumerford stood and said, "They may be pleased but no one will know what we've done here. The only report that will be written will be mine. It will, however, include praise for each of you. Prime Minister Pitt will surely read it and know what you've accomplished."

"As I expected," Donland said. "Another secret to be kept."

"You do understand," Sumerford said and clapped Donland on the shoulder.

"We best be away," Donland said and called to Hornsby, "Form the men up, Mister Hornsby, I shall take the lead and you the rear. Don't allow any man to slow the pace!"

"Aye, Captain!" Hornsby answered.

Chapter Twelve

Donland and Sumerford led the column of men up more hills and along a swamp. It took the better part of an hour to reach the coast. The trail opened then ended in a small fishing village. Two men watched as Donland and his party passed through the village. The women and children of the village hid inside the small thatched huts.

Oxford was sailing close-hauled about a half-mile at sea on a southern tack. She was the only ship visible

"How long before they see us?" Sumerford asked.

Donland ginned and said, "We've already been seen. Watch and you will see her go about and start to close. My guess is that she will put the boats over in less than an hour. Until then, we best set our defenses. We can expect the soldiers to come along the same track we traveled."

"What do you propose?" Sumerford asked.

"We will make our stand at the water's edge," Donland said and ordered Honest, "Take ten men and collect those three fishing boats, bring them down to the water's edge."

"Aye," Honest answered.

"Mister Hornsby, have the men start building a sand barricade that they can lay behind. Once done, make sure every pistol is loaded. We will lay the boats atop the barricade to provide protection."

"Aye, Captain," Hornsby replied.

"You expect them to attack?" Sumerford asked.

"Aye, if the ship is delayed we may have to defend ourselves and I'd rather prepare now than have to do so under fire," Donland answered.

He then turned his attention to *Oxford*; she was in the midst of going about. It was a comfort to know that he and the others would soon be under the protection of her guns.

His mouth was as dry as sand. The hot sun was bearing down and steam was rising for the tops of the thatched huts. He could only hope *Oxford's* boats would arrive before some of the men began slipping away in search of something to drink. They would prefer rum and would know that there would be a good chance to find some in one of the huts.

The fishing boats were brought and laid upon the sand barrier. Hornsby ordered the men to pack sand around the boats to make them secure.

Donland watched and once he was satisfied he ordered, "Every man behind the barricade," he shouted.

"Mister Hornsby, check the pistols, if you please. A loaded pistol with a barrel full of sand is of no use!"

"Aye, Captain," Hornsby answered.

"Honest, you help check the pistols!"

Oxford completed going about and was closing to the beach. As she drew nearer, Donland was able to make out that several of her forward gun-ports were open. Powell was not taking any chances and was prepared to respond if needed.

"Dark in a couple of hours," Honest remarked as he slumped down in the sand beside Donland.

"And it will be near that by the time we are back aboard," Donland replied.

"Think they will come, Captain?"

Donland rose up on one elbow and studied the village. "We can't know but if that Frenchman is as Sumerford claims, he will not rest until he has his revenge. You know just as I that a man like that will pursue at all costs. So, the sooner we are away from here the better."

"Aye," Honest said while studied *Oxford's* progress.

Sumerford lit another one of his cheroots.

Donland asked, "Do you agree with my assessment?"

Sumerford shifted his weight and answered, "Unfortunately, you are correct except the brunt of his anger will be directed at me. He will see my hand in all of this."

It occurred to Donland that he had not asked if the ships under construction were destroyed. "Were you successful in your endeavors?"

"I believe so," Sumerford said. "Your Mister Andrews is quite the fire-breather. He placed each one of the casks of powder directly under the keels and lit the fuses. Those vessels and the means to construct more were completely destroyed. While he was about planting the power the others torched the supplies, the buildings and anything that would burn. I doubt the rain mattered at all."

"Then we accomplished all you could hope for?" Donland asked.

"In a word, yes," Sumerford answered and puffed his cheroot.

They lay in the sand, watching and waiting. None of the villagers ventured from their huts. Here and there along the line of men lying in the sand there were jokes about the heat and their thirst. Donland sorely missed his hat.

"She's putting over the boats," Honest remarked.

Donland was pleased to see *Oxford's* remaining two small boats going over. Powell was in the process of reducing sail and it was apparent that he did not intend to lie-to. The crew of the boats would have a hard pull to catch up to *Oxford*.

"Mister Andrews, twelve men to a boat. Count them off, if you please!" Make use of the fishing boats!" Donland ordered. He added, "The wounded men first!"

"Aye, Captain!" Andrews answered.

Donland continued to watch the track for signs of approaching soldiers while the men were loaded into the boats. He held the men with muskets with him until all but one of the boats were away and then he and they sprinted to the water's edge.

The boats were so heavily loaded that water sloshed over the gunnels and forced the men not rowing to bail. None were left ashore. Poor Malcolm was unconscious and was being held up by two men. Donland prayed the young man would survive but he was almost certain to lose the leg.

There were no lanterns showing aboard *Oxford*. Donland stood in the stern with one hand upon Honest's shoulder for support as he issued commands to the boat's crew. The light was fading quickly, and the men pulled with all their strength attempting to catch up to the ship as she maintained steerage.

At last, exhausted men reached out to grasp *Oxford's* rope ladder. Donland ordered, "Tie on forward! Wounded away first!" It was not the normal order but Donland forsook tradition for expediency.

The second boat bumped into the stern of the first boat and began to tie on. Andrews followed Donland's example and ordered the wounded up the hull first. Night had fallen by the time the last man was up and over the hull.

"Any sightings?" Donland asked after returning Powell's salute.

Powell answered from the darkness, "There was movement in the bay but no ship has emerged."

"What of the wind?"

"We've the land breeze," Powell answered.

"Then let us make use of it and find deeper water. Set our course for due east; use as much sail as prudent. I am going to my cabin to scrub and a change of clothes."

"Aye, Captain," Powell acknowledged and asked, "Do these need to be fed?"

Donland had not considered food but at the mention of eating felt the pang. "Aye and a large tot of rum. Our people did well this day."

Rowland was prepared for Donland's return. The basin was filled and two towels were laid by. A clean and freshly pressed uniform was laid out as well. "Will you be need a shave?" Rowland inquired.

Donland ran his hand over his chin. "I think not but thank you Rowland."

"Rosita has prepared your dinner, Captain. Will you have it after you've dressed?"

"Aye," Donland answered as he stripped off the uniform coat and shirt. As an afterthought he said, "Pass the word for Mister Sumerford to join me for dinner."

"Aye, Captain," Rowland answered.

Sumerford had made use of water and a scrub brush. He arrived freshly shaven and in a clean shirt.

"Decent of you to invite me to dine," Sumerford stated.

"The pleasure is mine. I'm sure you are as hungry as I and could do with a brandy afterwards."

"Before and after, if you please."

Rowland was quick off the mark and poured a goodly amount into a glass while Sumerford seated himself.

"Thank you, Rowland," he said as he received the glass.

Rosita entered followed by her son. "On the platter she carried was a blackened roasted duck surrounded by potatoes and carrots. John, her son, held a platter of sliced bread, cheeses and butter.

Sumerford smiled and said, "There are benefits to being a captain."

"Aye," Donland agreed. "Providing one is fortunate enough to earn a little prize money along. Those who do not must contend with ship's fare."

"A personal cook and valet are also an added expensive are they not?"

"The cook, yes the valet, no. Rowland is carried on the muster as a seaman."

Sumerford took a long swallow of brandy and then reached for a slice of bread. Both men eyed the duck.

"Before we eat," Donland said.

Sumerford looked at him questionably.

"We survived an ordeal and I feel the need to say grace," Donland said and bowed his head.

He did not see Sumerford smile and bow his head.

Donland took the knife and sliced through the duck's breast. He then added potatoes and a few carrots. Filling his own plate was one of the tasks he did not allow Rowland or Rosita to do for him. Once he had said to them, "A man knows how much of whatever there is that he wants to eat. As Captain, I can make that judgment."

"You know he will come after me," Sumerford said.

"Aye, either on this voyage or at some later day. From what you've told me about him, I would expect no less. Perhaps an assassin?"

"Perhaps, he's been known to employ them when it suits his need. I confess that it will not be something that will cause me worry or to lie awake at night. I've more than my share of enemies that would relish the opportunity to drive home the blade."

"For king and country?" Donland mused.

Sumerford was honest, "Profit as well, I'll not deny it."

"And this venture, will you profit by it?"

Sumerford held his knife and fork over his plate and answered. "Yes, I was paid what I requested which was a considerable sum. But, I ask you, did they receive good value for their investment?"

Donland did not hesitate, "They did for there are many merchants that will hold fatter purses and there are many who serve the King that will not have to face so bold and powerful an enemy. The resources to contain such a squadron of ships would have been immense and you've accomplished it with a single vessel. So, yes, I would say the money, ever how much it was, was of little consequence."

Sumerford grinned. He said, "I knew you would see the value."

Donland lifted his glass of wine, held it for a moment then drank. "I've a question and call upon you as a friend to answer truthfully. Did you devise this plan with the inclusion of *Oxford* as your agent of choice?"

The air between them was heavy before Sumerford answered. "Isaac, there are few men I truly call friend and you are aware of that fact. There is but one man I trust with my life. You are that man. We have, as I told you on other occasions faced, storm, hunger and certain death together. There is no other on the face of the Earth that I can rely on so completely as you. So, in answer to your question, yes you were at the center of my plan. It was difficult to arrange the sending of Major Dormer to the Falklands but it was a necessary disguise to my plan and gave me the means to obtain your services. The capture of the sloop was a fortunate occurrence, which allowed you to devise the actual attack. Were it not for that sloop I am sure I would have had difficulty persuading you to put your ship at risk. In fact, you would have rebelled against the idea. But, in the end I would have given you no choice. Those ships had to be destroyed. You asked for the truth, now you have it."

"And what of Major Dormer?" Donland asked.

"Once I've reported our results, you will be dispatched to retrieve the major."

"I think it goes without saying that I will tell him nothing of your plan. He would not take kindly to having been a pawn in your scheme."

Sumerford burst into laughter. He laughed so hard he had to take out his handkerchief and wipe his eyes. He said, "No he would not, no more than you have taken kindly to it."

Donland chewed and drank. He mulled what Sumerford had said. He then stated, "From start to finish this plan of yours must have cost an enormous amount of money."

Sumerford merely said, "I was told I had absolute liberty."

"They trust you that much?" Donland asked.

Sumerford laid down his fork and knife and answered, "They had no choice. The price I was paid and all the expenditures were far and away less than the cost in lives and material of a war. Pitt is no fool and he knows me not to be one."

"Another friend?" Donland asked.

"More than friend," Sumerford answered.

Donland did not press further. He was aware that there were some things in life that were dangerous to know.

Chapter Thirteen

Donland opened his watch; it read five till five. He closed it and shoved his foot into the boot. The gray of morning out the galley window showed no inkling of sunrise.

"Rosita is preparing your breakfast," Honest reported and added, "Rowland is brushing your hat and coat."

"Aye and what of the deck?"

"Gray morning, light airs, Mister Powell ordered that we lie-to."

"Just as well," Donland responded.

"Dawn in about an hour."

"Aye," Donland replied as Rowland came in bearing a pitcher of water and a razor.

"I hope you have stropped it well this morning," Donland said as Rowland placed a towel around Donland's neck.

"Aye, Captain, sharper than yesterday," Rowland answered and began preparing the soap.

The shaving was one thing that Rowland insisted upon doing. He and Donland reached agreement on most things but having a valet was something to which Donland was totally unaccustomed. Like many seamen, Rowland was a pressed man. He was from Devonshire and a family of servants. As a lad of fifteen he tired of the servant life and set out on his own for America. Unfortunately for him, he was caught and pressed. For three years he served as an ordinary seaman aboard a brig before it was sold off. Starving, he stowed aboard a merchant vessel and landed almost as starved in Jamaica. Honest came across him outside a pub, took pity on him and brought him aboard *Oxford* to be Donland's valet. "He can do for you better than I can," Honest stated and Donland agreed.

Rosita set a plate of ham and beans with fresh bread and butter before Donland. The coffee was made from freshly ground beans and was flavored the way Donland liked it with honey.

Breakfast was interrupted by a knock at the door. The surgeon, Doctor Trammel, entered. "Beg pardon for intruding on your breakfast but I thought I should come before your day becomes cluttered. It concerns young Malcolm, he wishes to see you."

Donland asked, "How is he?"

"Not well but I believe he will recover. It will take time and he is very weak."

"What of the leg, did you remove it?"

Trammel's face wrinkled, and he replied, "Not as yet, it has color and doesn't smell putrid. I would guess it has a chance to heal. Another day and I'll know."

"And why does he want to see me?"

"He did not tell me but I had to promise that I would come to you. Whatever it is, it is something he does not want to take to his grave."

Donland smiled at that. "Doctor Trammel there are any number of things that none of us want to take to the grave. However, I will come round, you can tell him."

"Very good Sir, it will do the lad good to know that you are coming," Trammel said.

"Is there anything else?"

"No, that is all," Trammel answered while eyeing the ham.

Donland could not help but notice the staring so he said, "Do sit Doctor Trammel and eat, there is more than enough for the two of us. Will you have coffee?"

"Coffee? Dear Sir, yes and thank you!"

Doctor Trammel consumed the rest of the ham and sopped the bit of gravy. "Most wonderful," he said as he downed the remaining coffee.

"Then let us go below and see what has so occupied Mister Malcolm's mind." Donland said as he rose.

Rowland helped him on with his coat and handed him his hat.

Donland asked, "You did not see Rio de Janeiro, disappointed?"

Trammel replied, "Yes, and no. I've not been aboard a man-of-war before and observed her in battle. Given the choice of a visit to the city or the experience of battle, I would have chosen to visit the city. However, being aboard and experiencing the power of those big guns is something I will long remember."

"Better to experience them on this side of the muzzles than the other," Donland said.

Trammel faced him and said, "That is so, Captain. I'd not want to do so and pray that I am never on the other side of them. Have you been on the other side?"

Donland half-smiled and said, "Aye, and more than once. Let us not talk about it. You do understand?"

"I do, memories are not always pleasant," Trammel said.

Malcolm lay in the hammock under a blanket. The young man's face was covered in sweat and he brushed it away from his eyes.

"How is it with you Mister Malcolm," Donland asked.

The young man smiled, his red hair was plastered to his head. "Better, Captain, much better," he answered.

"Why the blanket?" Donland asked.

Trammel answered, "Sweat, Sir, to sweat the poisons out of him. I've given him a lot of water with a good measure of salt. Sweating has been proven to aid in recovery. I don't know how it manages to do it but it does."

"You asked to see me Mister Malcolm," Donland said as he turned back to the young man.

"Aye, Captain, I wanted to thank you, they would surely have killed me if you had not taken them when you did."

Donland smiled in the lantern light and said, "I confess I did not know it was you and was pleased to find that it was you we rescued. I'd not want to lose my most promising young officer."

Malcolm replied, "Thank you, I'd not want to disappoint you." His face clouded over. After a moment he said, "I did not do my duty."

"How so, Mister Malcolm? What did you fail to do?"

Malcolm's face against twisted as if in pain. He said, "I was afraid, Sir, mortally afraid and did not lead my men in the fight when the soldiers started firing at us. It was left to Billings to rally the men."

Donland nodded and said, "Many an officer when faced with an unexpected situation will hesitate. When Billings rallied the men, what did you do?"

"I fired my pistol at one of the soldiers."

"Did you hit him?"

"Aye, Captain, square in the chest. I'll not forget his face."

Donland nodded again and said, "You hesitated and recovered taking down one of your attackers. There was no neglect of duty, rest easy now. Follow the surgeon's instructions for I will need you to stand your watch as soon as he releases you. Think no more of the incident and I will record your bravery in my report."

"But, Captain!" Malcolm cried.

"You proved your mettle, Mister Malcolm and as I said, that is what I will state in my report. Let this be the end of it."

Meekly Malcolm answered, "Aye, Captain."

Once they were away from Malcolm, Donland said to Honest in a whisper, "Seek out Billings and inquire about the action. Do so in a way that does not reflect on Mister Malcolm."

"Aye, Captain," Honest answered.

They climbed the ladder to the quarterdeck and were greeted with a gray morning. Donland checked the compass and studied the set of the sails. Andrews had the watch.

"Have you a lookout?" Donland asked.

"Not as yet, Captain," Andrews answered.

"Then I suggest you send two men up."

"Aye, Captain!"

"Mister Welles send Bill and Anson to the trees," Andrews ordered.

"Aye," David answered and hurried down the ladder to the waist to find the two men.

Winslow heaved his bulk on to his perch and appeared to be chewing on a biscuit.

"Mister Winslow what of the wind?" Donland asked.

"A south wind, Captain once the sun comes over the horizon; you can feel it on your check, can you not?"

"Aye," Donland answered and turned to gaze into the gray. Something troubled him, and he realized what it was. "Mister Winslow, this south wind is it fair from Río de Janeiro?"

"Aye, it is, Captain," Winslow answered.

A sudden realization struck Donland as hard as a fist in the gut. "Mister Andrews call all hands, beat to quarters!"

"Aye, Captain," Andrews said without questioning.

Oxford's deck came alive, and whistles shrieked and the bell clanged. The drummer boy wiped sleep from his eyes and began to beat out the rhythmic call to quarters.

Powell bounded up the ladder to the quarterdeck seconds later with his coat unbuttoned and attempted to buckle on his sword.

"Where away," he called before he saw Donland standing by the railing in the faint light.

Donland turned and said, "Belay, Mister Powell,"

He then called, "Hands to the braces!"

"Take out mains'sl reefs!"

He turned back to Powell and said, "Wind is aft of us Mister Powell, gather all the wind and make haste, we've no time to lose!"

"Mister Winslow, steer due north!" Donland ordered.

"Aye, Captain!"

Donland craned his neck, cupped his hands and called up to the lookouts, "Sharp eye aft!"

Bill called down, "Aye, Captain."

"What are you about?" Sumerford, shoeless and shirtless, demanded as he came toward Donland.

"Your Frenchman," Donland said and explained, "He'll not rest!"

Sumerford stammered, "My God man its still night!"

"Aye," Donland said. "But the wind favors him and I believe that he ordered his ship warped out of the bay by boats and even now has filled his sail and as soon as the sun hits our sails will tack to bring us to action."

Sumerford's face registered the truth of Donland's words.

Donland pressed on, "As I said, your Frenchman will not rest if his hatred of you is as great as you say and his lust for revenge is as consuming as you suggest."

Andrews interrupted, "Beg pardon Captain, are the guns to be loaded?"

The question did not come as a surprise but it required an appropriate answer, one that he, until that moment, had not contemplated fully. "The crews are to stand to their guns and have all in readiness. We are not at war but we will defend ourselves if necessary."

"Aye, Captain," Andrews replied with a questioning look on his face and turned to the ladder.

Donland called after him, "Mister Aldridge will assume Mister Malcolm's duties."

"Aye, Captain!" Andrews replied as he continued on his way below.

Men worked aloft removing the gaskets to unfurl the sails, those on the deck were hauling on the braces. Their tasks required little light after so many years of afloat in all extremes of weather.

Donland paced the deck waiting and watching the sky. There was little more to be done until there was light so he paced and watched the sky. No one interfered with his pacing or spoke to him. It was on his fourth circuit of the quarterdeck that he realized that it was getting lighter; he could make out men moving about on the foredeck.

Honest tapped Donland lightly on the shoulder, leaned in and whispered, "Billings said that Mister Malcolm did his duty, he saw no slackness."

Donland smiled and said, "As I thought, only a moment, that moment that fear grips a man."

"Aye," Honest said and stepped back.

"Hands in the chains Mister Powell!" Donland ordered.

The words were no sooner out of his mouth that the lookout called, "Deck there! Sail aft!"

The sighting was expected but unsettling.

Winslow said with a touch of humor, "We've not our britches around our ankles."

"She'll be miles behind us," Powell observed.

"Aye, Mister Powell and as long as this wind holds she'll have no chance to gain on us," Donland said and smiled.

"What made you suspect that we would be pursued?" Powell asked.

Donland replied, "There are those whose anger knows no limits. Add to such anger the cunning of a fox then you must be prepared for all possibilities. I was so filled with our success that I failed to remember that lesson I learned long ago. I could have prepared but did not and almost left it too late."

"But, you didn't and now we have the advantage," Powell said with a hint of a smile.

"That may be so but until we anchor, we must be on our guard. Pass the word, if you please, to Mister Andrews to stand down the guns."

"Aye," Powell answered.

Donland began pacing the quarterdeck again, occasionally glancing skyward. It was now light enough to see the entire deck. He stopped, pursed his lips and called, "Mister Powell, I'll have the stun'sls if you please!"

"Aye, Captain!" Powell answered and lifted his speaking trumpet. "Rig for stun'sls!"

His order instigated a sudden rush and patter of feet. Men climbed into the shrouds and others hauled the necessary tackle from lockers.

"Lively there!" Brunson shouted.

"You there! Move your arse!"

Donland resumed his pacing, as the deck became a beehive of activity.

Andrews approached Donland and reported, "All guns secured, Captain!"

Donland nodded and said, "Take over the mizzen from Mister Hornsby. No slackness, Mister Andrews."

"Aye, Captain," Andrews replied.

"Four knots!" Brunson shouted as he relayed the speed from the man in the chains.

"We'll have five out of her when the stun'sls start to draw!" Powell declared.

"Near to six, I would think with this wind, it should be enough to keep us well ahead of that seventy-four," Donland said.

The sky was clear of cloud except for some high wisps. *Oxford* held her course with all sails billowing. The French seventy-four was a beautiful sight as her sails too billowed like clouds upon the sea. She was some miles aft and was unable to close the distance. Mister Aldridge watched, as the last grains of sand trickled down the hourglass. "The glass is turned!" he shouted.

"Note it in the log, Mister Aldridge," Brunson ordered.

"Aye, Sir," Aldridge answered and rang the bell twice before moving to make the entry into the logbook.

Sumerford sat across from Donland's desk puffing one of his cheroots and holding a glass of brandy. Honest sat with his chair tilted back against the bulkhead and dozed.

"One o'clock," Donland remarked without looking up from the stores logbook. The figures entered by the purser, Leeland matched his own.

"I'm for some air," Sumerford announced as he sat his glass on the sideboard.

"Aye," Donland said and closed the log.

"Wind's dying, it's fitful and waning and a bit coming from the west," Winslow announced as Donland came near.

A sail on the mizzen flapped loudly and Andrews ordered, "Another pull on that brace!"

Donland snatched a glass from the rack and stepped to the larboard gunnel. He found the seventy-four without effort and observed that her sails billowed with the strain of wind. She was a half-mile or more eastward than *Oxford* and appeared to be on a more eastward tack. "The Frenchman is faring better than we are he's better wind," he said.

"Mister Brunson, how many knots?" he asked.

"Four, Sir," Brunson answered.

Donland studied the sea; it was as calm as could be expected. Without the shadow of clouds to mar the surface he was able to discern the passing of wind currents.

"Mister Winslow, what of the afternoon?"

"Wind is going to be fitful, barometer is rising. There may be a wind coming off the coast by the second dogwatch, doldrums before that," Winslow answered.

"Deck there two sails, larboard bow!" the lookout shouted.

Donland lifted the glass he was holding and scanned the horizon. He didn't see the sails.

"Mister Aldridge, up to the masthead, if you please and see what your young eyes can discover," Donland ordered.

"Aye, Captain," Aldridge answered and jerked a glass from the rack.

Donland watched the young man climb and remembered the days of his youth when he could climb like Aldridge. He had been just as swift and unconcerned about the dizzying height; unconcerned about the dangers aboard a man-of-war. His conversation with Trammel tugged at his mind and was replaced with an image of Malcolm being afraid when the soldiers attacked. He shook off the thoughts, now was not the time to remember being so young.

"Friend or foe, do suppose?" Sumerford asked.

"We have no foes for we are not at war," Donland answered.

"Ah, but we are in a sense, do not forget that we are being hunted from behind," Sumerford said.

"I've not forgotten but other than one angry man we have nothing to fear from any other vessel we encounter."

"There's always the possibility of a war having been declared," Sumerford reminded him. "We've been away for several months."

"That is true," Donland said. "But, no matter what the nationality of those vessels, we will render appropriate honors. I will cause those captains no needless concern. However, the guns below deck will be manned and at the ready."

"A sensible precaution," Sumerford said.

Overhead sails began to flap as the wind was dying.

"Braces there!" Powell shouted.

"Wind's going," Winslow said as he slid off his perch.

"They're becalmed!" Aldridge shouted down.

"Can you make them out?" Donland shouted up.

Several seconds passed before Aldridge called down, "French flag on the gaff!"

Donland said as much to himself as to Sumerford, "We've nothing to fear from them." A thought struck him and he said, "I'm going up!" He removed his hat and handed it to Welles and then unbuttoned his coat.

"Come down Mister Aldridge," he called up as he reached up to climb the shroud.

"Aye, Captain," Aldridge answered and began to descend.

Donland took his time climbing. He was about halfway when he passed the younger man. "Your glass, if you please, Mister Aldridge."

Clinging to the rope with one hand, Aldridge used the other to remove the lanyard from his neck and handed over the telescope.

Donland reached the topmast yard and sucked in gulps of air. He had not climbed the mast in a long time and took note of how age had changed him. The two French ships were but large dots to his naked eye. He hugged the mast with his arms to free his hands to hold the glass and began to search for the ships. The larger ship appeared to be a transport and the smaller of the two, he decided, was a small frigate of no more than thirty guns. It was as he expected. Next he pivoted on the mast and found the seventy-four. She was beginning to have difficulties and her sails were flapping in the failing wind. She had, however, decreased the distance between them.

Looking down from the great height, *Oxford's* deck appeared a lot smaller and the men no more than midgets. He began the climb down, which was not nearly as taxing as the climb up had been.

"Mister Powell," Donland said as he slipped an arm into his coat, "I'll have the boats put over and manned, if you please. It will be hot work but I mean to increase the distance between *Oxford* and that seventy-four."

"We still have a bit of wind," Powell stated.

"Aye, we do and we will make the best use of it possible," Donland said and turned to Winslow, "Mister Winslow, set our course north by west."

"Aye, Captain," Winslow answered.

Sumerford asked, "Is this a wise move, I've heard you speak about the danger of a lee shore? We are near enough to the coast that even I can see it."

"Wind, Mister Sumerford, it is always about the wind when you are at sea. If you have it you can maneuver, if you don't then you are at the mercy of those who do. I plan to be the one with the wind and there will be a land breeze before there is a stirring this far from the land."

"You mean to leave that Portuguese ship well behind, is that your plan?"

"Aye it is, and the more distance between the better. If we are becalmed, then we become a temptation. We've no reason to linger," Donland said and faced the seventy-four.

"Haul!" Brunson shouted to the men hoisting the first boat.

Oxford responded to her rudder as Winslow gave orders to the helmsman.

The linesman in the chains casting the log shouted, "Two knots!"

Donland heard and checked the sails, only the royals remained full. The wind was dying fast.

Powell lifted his speaking trumpet and ordered, "Brace round, Mister Hornsby! Hold all the wind you can!"

Everything that could be done to capture and hold more wind was being done. When it died, and would do so in minutes, all four vessels would be left to sit and roll until wind returned.

The wind died completely just as the second boat was lowered. "Give way all!" Aldridge, who commanded the first boat called.

Seconds later the second boat commanded by Welles followed the first. They rowed to *Oxford's* bow and waited to receive their respective hawsers.

Donland watched the boats row out beyond the bows and the hawsers tighten. *Oxford* was no small sloop that could be easily nudged. However, with the way still on the ship, the extra pull of the boats would maintain steerage for some minutes. After that, it would be the brute force applied to the oars than would bring any movement.

Without wind, the heat bore down unmercifully. Donland was sweating and considered removing his hat but decided to wait. He would bear the coat a little longer. He lifted the telescope and focused on the seventy-four. Her sails lay limp. It would not be long before whoever commanded her would realize that *Oxford* had boats in the water. As difficult as it was to tow *Oxford* it would be even more difficult to move a ship the size of the seventy-four.

"One knot!" the linesman called.

"Mister Powell!" Donland called.

"Captain," Powell answered as he came up the ladder from the waist.

"Have the captured fishing boat put over and rotate some men every half-hour," Donland ordered.

"Aye, Captain," Powell said and nodded.

"And James, you can remove your coat," Donland added and smiled. "We've a hot afternoon."

"Aye," Powell replied.

Chapter Fourteen

"Bit of cloud just off the starboard bow," Winslow stated.
Donland had noticed the hit of cloud a few minutes earlier.
He was also aware of the widening gap between the seventy-four
and *Oxford*.

The bell clanged once signaling the start of the dogwatch. It
appeared that Winslow was to be correct as to when the land
breeze would arrive. Since *Oxford* was closer inshore than the
other three vessels she would receive it first. It would give her
the opportunity to be underway and moving before the others.

The heat bore down melting the tar in the rigging. Donland,
wearing only his shirt, hat and britches mounted the steps to the
poop. He carried with him the ship's most powerful telescope to
see what if anything the captain of the Portuguese ship was
doing? The first thing that caught his eye was a boat in the water.
He smiled to himself as he thought of those men laboring to
haul their ship giving chase to *Oxford*. The smile left his face as
he realized that something was not quite right. He shifted his
stance and refocused the glass. He couldn't see it! As hard as he

tried he could not see a hawser. Shifting again, he focused on a second boat, there was no hawser.

He stood and rubbed his eye while still studying the ship. His brain flashed a message, "there is no hawser that long!" Those boats were not attempting to tow their ship; no they were loaded with men to attack *Oxford*! "Fools" Donland exclaimed.

"Mister Powell, recall our boats! There are boarders coming to us!" Donland ordered as he regained the quarterdeck.

Powell's face reflected confusion but he replied, "Aye, Captain."

"Mister Vickers, Pass the word for Mister Sharpe and Mister Brunson."

"Aye," the youngster replied and set off to find the two officers.

"Is something a foot, Captain?" Honest asked.

"Aye, it is, Honest." Donland answered.

Donland rubbed his chin, looked to the west to see how near the clouds were. They would not arrive in time; he would have to do what was necessary. It was not to his liking.

Sharpe clambered up the hatch ladder and onto the quarterdeck. "Captain, you sent for me?"

"Aye, Mister Sharpe, I've work for you and your lads. There are three boats approaching us from aft. Load the three pounders with grape and mount the swivels. I'll leave it to you to fire when you deem it is time."

"Aye, Captain," Sharpe answered with a hint of glee.

"Captain?" Brunson said as he stepped beside Sharpe.

"We are being pursued, Mister Brunson. I'll have our aft guns loaded and run out. You may fire when the boats are in range. Lieutenant Sharpe and his men will man the poop."

"Aye, Captain!" Andrews answered.

"No quarter, Gentlemen," Donland said as the two men turned to go.

The first man over the side was Welles followed by the men who crewed the boat towing *Oxford*. Donland called to him, "Well done Mister Welles!"

The way came off *Oxford* and she lay wallowing on the rollers. The heat seemed to double. "No steerage!" Winslow called.

Powell came up from the waist. "Arm our men, Mister Powell! Station them on the gunnels to repel boarders!" Donland ordered.

"Aye, Captain," Powell answered.

"Boats are less than a half-mile out, Captain," Sharpe called down from the poop.

"Fire when they are in range, Mister Sharpe!"

"Aye, Captain!"

The cloud bank was drawing nearer and was darkening. Winslow noticed Donland staring at it and remarked, "We'll have the wind but not the gales. Rain will die out before it reaches us."

"The wind is all I require, Mister Winslow," Donland responded.

The sudden distant boom of a cannon caught Donland by surprise. Seconds after the sound came the smashing and crashing of glass as the ball through the stern galley windows.

"They've a gun in one of the boats!" Powell shouted.

The shot was well aimed and blasted through along the upper gun deck.

"See to the damage, Mister Andrews!" Powell shouted as he leaned out over the gunnel to glimpse the boats.

"Gun one ready!" A marine on the poop shouted.

"Fire!" Lieutenant Sharpe answered, and the three-pounder boomed like thunder. It was followed by one of the nine pounders on the upper gun deck.

"Huzza!" "Huzza!" Came shouts from the poop.

"They've hit one of the boats!" Powell exclaimed.

"Aye," Donland said. His thoughts were on the second gun that Brunson commanded. Perhaps the shot into the galley had wrecked it.

"Fire!" Sharpe commanded and the second three-pounder exploded filling the air in the direction of one of the boats with grape-shot.

"Captain! Beg pardon, Sir, Mister Andrews' compliments. One gun is out of action. Mister Brunson was wounded and Mister Andrews has taken command."

Muskets began to crack on the poop and another of the three-pounders sent a swarm of angry buzzing grape into one of the boats.

There came an answering boom as a gun on one of the boats fired. The ball went wide and landed a few feet away from *Oxford's* hull.

Powell's men were now leaning out over the gunnel firing muskets.

"Fire!" Sharpe's voice carried over the pop and muskets banged on the poop. The swivels unleashed a torrent of buzzing mini-balls.

Donland was about to ascend the ladder to the poop when a mizzen sail flapped. He watched as it filled and twist slightly. The bank of clouds was coming quickly.

"They're turning back!" Sharpe shouted. "Give the buggers another round!"

It was what Donland wanted to hear. He called above the bark of the muskets, "Mister Powell, prepare to get underway!"

Powell stepped away from the gunnel and gazed up at the sails, then replied, "Aye Captain!"

The sudden rush of wind rocked *Oxford*.

"Lay us on a north by east course, Mister Winslow," Donland ordered.

"Aye, Captain!"

"Mister Powell, hands aloft!"

"Captain," Lieutenant Andrews called as he came onto the quarterdeck. "I've secured the guns. We've two casualties, I've sent Mister Brunson to the surgeon, he's a small splinter in his back."

"See to your division, Mister Andrews!" Donland ordered.

Oxford gathered the wind into her sails.

"Steerage!" Winslow called.

"Steer aft of the French frigate," Donland ordered.

"Aye, Captain," Winslow answered.

Sharpe bounded down the poop ladder, "They've given it up, Captain," he reported with a grin. "Our lads gave it to em' good!"

"It was a fool's last hurrah," Donland said.

"Aye, it was Sir, but putting that gun in the boat was a nice touch."

"That it was Mister Sharpe; I'd not expected that captain doing it."

Donland turned to Honest, "Go to the gaff to render honors to the French. Wait for the gun!"

"Aye, Captain," Honest answered.

"One last task, Mister Sharpe, one gun to signal honors, wait for my order," Donland said and smiled.

"Aye, Sir, but have we not already signaled honor?"

"No, Mister Sharpe, we have not, honor to whom honor is due and death to them that it is owed. We are at peace with the French and will render honors accordingly."

"Aye, Captain!"

"Peace," Sumerford said as he lit one of his cheroots, "is just an intermission in the killing."

"Aye," Donland replied and added, "But for the sailor it is time to shed the sea, hold a woman and rest his soul."

Sumerford smiled, "And, I know the woman that waits for you."

Epilouge

The pale yellow house overlooked Charleston's harbor. On the widow's walk stood Betty Sumerford watching as *Oxford* tacked under top'sls' to her anchorage. The wind was cold and she was wrapped in her cloak. Tears, not from the wind, but of joy streamed down her cheeks. The letter she received from Antigua stated that *Oxford* would arrive before Christmas on her return from the Falklands. Arrangements were to be made to purchase a suitable home in the city and she was to prepare it to be their home.

Printed in Great Britain
by Amazon